THE SPY GAME

THE SPY GAME

MARC LOVELL

PUBLISHED FOR THE CRIME CLUB BY
DOUBLEDAY & COMPANY, INC.
GARDEN CITY, NEW YORK
1980

All of the characters in this book
are fictitious, and any resemblance
to actual persons, living or dead,
is purely coincidental.

ISBN: 0-385-17073-4
Library of Congress Catalog Card Number 80-499
Copyright © 1980 by Doubleday & Company, Inc.
All Rights Reserved
Printed in the United States of America
First Edition

THE SPY GAME

ONE

You can always tell a spook, Apple was thinking. He's the one who walks into a place at his ease, as if it wasn't his first visit but the hundredth. He doesn't try to look everywhere at once. He doesn't pat pockets or fidget with his tie or touch his nose. Your spook is so casual it wasn't true. No one had that much self-assurance.

This information was the latest in the string that Appleton Porter had been dredging out of his memory all afternoon. There were hundreds of bits and pieces. He had learned them during Training Four or had picked them up from other agents. The data were all theory. Apple himself, he had never been out in the espionage field.

Which is why he was excited; why he sat tense and alert on the bus that was heading for Trafalgar Square.

I'm being childish, Apple mused. And, apropos, wasn't that inevitable nose-touching the adult version of the stressful little boy grabbing his crotch? Probably. But that was changing the topic.

Yes, he admitted, he was being childish. He was excited at the prospect of playing spy.

Defensively, Appleton Porter pulled out cigarettes. He remembered he was on the lower, no-smoking deck of the bus. He rose and went upstairs. The physical action was a relief.

He lit a cigarette and hoped he didn't look mysterious. He also hoped he did.

Apple looked mundane. He looked six feet seven inches of thin, middle-class Englishman, as mysterious as bitten fingernails. His sandy hair was Establishment in neatness and length, his pale face acceptably good-looking. His keen green eyes were his best feature: they helped people disregard the freckles.

He was wearing, as usual, a dark suit with a pattern of small checks; he felt it served to reduce his height and lessen the thinness. He would have preferred larger, louder checks but that wasn't in his public nature; the robe he wore at home was a screaming tartan.

Apple was his customary tidy self, and he despaired of it all. He was glad of this afternoon's anomaly, the bulge under his left armpit.

Apple had been allied to the Intelligence organisations since leaving university eight years ago, a star in Modern Languages. He spoke six fluently, another five with competence but an accent, and had a working knowledge of seven more. He was a senior official at the UK Philological Institute, where no one knew of his other rôle.

Not that that rôle took up much of his time. It was an occasional thing. He checked decoded transcriptions for nuance and word-play; at high-level military conferences he did that most difficult of tasks, simultaneous translation; he wrote love and other letters in whatever phrasing was called for, polished or ungrammatical.

Apple was like many other faceless agents attached to the secret services, each man with a speciality that might be needed no more than once a year, from safe-breaker to lip-reader, from acrobat to hypnotist. He was invaluable— once in a while.

Apple had never lost his glamorous view of the cloak-and-dagger world. He used its slang. He was a fan of spy fiction. Although he might live and dress as a bourgeois, inside him lurked a counter-culture, anti-hero, kitchen-sink, amoral rebel who was an inch over six feet tall and had broad shoulders, who was a boozer, a womaniser and a tough guy, and who never for a moment had looked like escaping.

Apple drew deeply on his cigarette, letting out the smoke again with a sigh. He knew it was more than child-ish to be excited about what lay ahead. It was pointless. The job was low on the scale—a courier—and would last fifteen minutes at the outside. You could hardly call it going out in the field. But he would anyway, because it was probably the nearest he would ever get.

Intelligence circles being as gossipy as any convention of psychologists, Apple had learned within his first year of semi-service how he rated as an agent. He could quote the dossier verbatim.

He scored ten out of ten for languages and security clearance, six for unarmed combat, acting ability and in-ventiveness in lies, five for resistance to body pain but nine in the mental variety, nine in general knowledge, marksmanship and memory, five in tolerance for alcohol.

Those low marks, Apple felt, could have been over-come, one way or another, with faking and practice and the pulling of strings. But there was no chance of getting around what came under the heading of Remarks. That was damning for all time, unless there was a personality change as well as shrinkage.

Not only was Appleton Porter too tall for successful dimming of presence, Remarks said, but he had a sympa-thetic nature, and blushed easily.

Apple blushed now—at the thought of how many people had read his dossier. Read and snickered. Read and passed the word on. Good old Russet Appleton.

Apple attacked the blush with the method he was currently using, which he had bought through an ad in a magazine. He pictured himself lying dead in a snowdrift. It worked. His face cooled and paled.

He drew on the cigarette, feeling cheerful. He ignored that this new method would surely lose its power within a week, as had all the others, stretching back to his painful teens.

At that time, a doctor had told Apple that he needed the confidence of an accomplishment, that he ought to take music lessons or learn a language; the more proficient he became at his choice, the less of a blusher he would be. Apple had believed the doctor, and to some extent still did. He had no ear for music.

The bus squealed to a stop. It stood throbbing like an exhausted animal. People clattered down the stairs, others came up. The bus lurched away. There were two more stops to go.

So as not to feel excited, Apple thought about how this mission had started. After lunch, the telephone had rung in his office at the Institute. The voice was Angus Watkin's, though he gave a number instead of a name. He asked, "Can you talk?"

"Yes, sir."

"I'll say this once, then you'll repeat it to me, then I'll ring off and get back to my tea. Clear?"

"Clear, sir."

"This afternoon a messenger will deliver to you a ticket for Batewell Hall. You will take it with you when you go to Trafalgar Square. There, at six o'clock, you will find a man with a train ticket in his hatband and a newspaper folded down to the crossword puzzle. Half the puzzle will be completed, in red ball-point. The signals are as follows."

It went on for three minutes. Apple had no trouble remembering details. After repeating everything, he asked, "What next, sir?"

"There is no next, Porter. Good afternoon."

But it was better than nothing, Apple thought now, and you never knew—this, if he performed well, could lead to other missions.

Why Apple had been chosen to play courier was, he knew, simply explained. His cover was perfect. He was unknown to the Intelligence forces of any other country. He didn't look like a field operative.

London, at this moment, was as full of agents as had been Lisbon during World War Two. Russians, Israelis, Americans, French, West Germans, freebooters—they were here under every shade of cover from tourist to embassy attaché. The KGB's job was protective.

At the Royal Festival Hall was appearing the latest cultural exchange, the Soviet Folk Dancers. At Batewell Hall, where an international parapsychological congress was being held, a group of Russians was demonstrating ESP. There were upward of a hundred U.S.S.R. nationals to be chaperoned.

Apple knew that everyone in espionage was watching the KGB, who were watching everyone else. There were circles of shadowers being shadowed. All British Intelligence buildings were under surveillance, for other powers knew exactly where they were, just as MI5 had floor plans of KGB Moscow headquarters, in addition to the plumber's materials estimate for that leaking cistern in the basement kitchen. This week, therefore, a known British agent would find his movements tightly restricted.

The bus brakes began to squeal. It was the last stop for Apple. He left his seat and went downstairs. His excitement was under control.

The bus stopped. As Apple stepped down from the platform he told himself he would play this to the pro hilt. He would be so self-assured and casual it wouldn't be true.

He crossed the road into Trafalgar Square. He touched his lapel, he thumbed his tie, he ran a forefinger under his nose.

"Nelson's Column is one hundred and sixty-two feet high, ladies and gentlemen. The material is granite, the style Corinthian. Those bas-reliefs at the base, depicting the battles of Aboukir, Copenhagen, St. Vincent and Trafalgar, were cast from the bronze of captured French cannon. The four lions that stand on guard, they were designed by Sir Edwin Landseer. Shall we take a closer look at those battle scenes?"

The guide led his group of tourists on. They were soon lost among the people and pigeons that crowded the two-acre square. Apple felt equally lost.

It was ten minutes to six. He had only a short time to pinpoint his man from among hundreds. He didn't know whether to be glad of that or not.

Not, he decided quickly, if future missions depended on him shining here. Only one skill was asked of the courier, the man who appears briefly at the midnight cross-roads and is never seen again: the skill of being punctual.

With relief, Apple remembered, *Always be, and believe*

yourself to be, one of the herd. Which meant that the operative he was to meet would be at the densest part of the crowd, and expect that to be realised by the courier.

Apple went toward the nearest cluster of pigeon-feeders. He was working on the assumption that the agent would be between thirty and fifty. He would, of course, be wearing a hat. Apple had been told nothing about the man, except that he had been recalled from abroad and would be coming here direct from the terminus, thus avoiding all usual Intelligence people and places.

The cluster contained women, children and two old men, the last pair hatless. Apple moved on around the column. He wondered about the granite used in its construction. Did it come from the same source as that used to build New Scotland Yard, quarried by convicts on Dartmoor? He also wondered why his mind had this fondness for the irrelevant, to mention nothing of the trivial.

There were two youngish men with hats in the next gathering. The rest were nuns and teen-age girls. Pigeons were thick on the ground and in the air.

Approaching, Apple put a hand into the left side of his jacket. He ended the bulge there by bringing out a bag of corn. Scattering feed, he circled the cluster. There was nothing in the men's hatbands.

Apple went on. He resisted the urge to look at his watch, which he had set to the second from the BBC. He wasn't waiting for anyone. He was out for a stroll on this fine September evening. He was one of the herd.

The rush of noise made Apple duck and almost cry out. His heart thumped an extra beat. It was only when he had swung around that he saw the pigeons. They were coming back for a second swoop. He diverted them by tossing the bag of corn away. Unnerved, he walked on quickly.

Apple made a full circuit of the lion-guarded pillar, conning groups of people but not ignoring loners. Remarkably few men wore headgear, and there were more caps than hats. He arrived back at the nuns and their charges. One of the men had gone.

Apple knew it had to be close to six o'clock, if not after. About to hurry away, he paused when the remaining man took off his hat. After running a hand over his hair, he put the hat on again. Now a sliver of ticket was showing above the band.

Style, Apple thought, relaxing cheerfully. He gave ten to the man, who was about his own age, average height and physique, sallow-faced and verging on being ugly. His suit needed pressing and a sweat stain rimmed his collar. He looked as if he hadn't sold a vacuum cleaner in days.

Realising that he was staring, Apple strolled off. He returned within seconds, but from the cluster's other side.

The man now had a small-folded newspaper in one hand, a pen in the other. But he wasn't looking at the paper, which he held at chin level; he was watching the more nubile of the teen-age girls.

Blinking with admiration, Apple awarded another ten. He was glad they were on the same team. How could anyone suspect a man of pretending not to be an operative when he was so intently pretending not to be an ogler of jail-bait?

Apple stepped back, changed his angle of vision. The paper's crossword puzzle had a scattering of words—in red ink. He moved to stand level with the man and some four feet away. Quietly he said:

"The domestic pigeon is pretty, but a nuisance."

"For Christ's sake," the man said in a weary tone. "Do we have to go through all that crap?"

His neck was broken and his lifeless eyes stared out of the snowdrift, which had long since frozen the blood from his wounds into hard, black clots.

Apple clung to the picture. It kept threatening to fade under the competition from his feelings. The blush was a scorcher. With a simple sentence, the agent had reduced him to the status of a schoolboy.

Apple stood on with his face turned the other way. When cool came, it was partly from the snowdrift, partly from recalling: *Never presume that a contact is all that he seems to be.*

He turned back to the man, who hadn't changed his stance, and who said, "You must be Russet Appleton."

Stiffly, plodding the words: "The domestic pigeon is pretty, but a nuisance."

The man sighed. "They don't do any real damage."

"Nelson wouldn't agree."

"No. He's one of the few seafaring names never to have needed whitewashing."

Which phrase, Apple knew, had to be of Angus Watkin's own making. He rarely missed a chance, no matter how oblique, to get in a dig at Naval Intelligence.

Apple no longer felt like a schoolboy. The man's initial response, he had realised, could have been a test for the neophyte. If so, it had been passed with all flags up.

Still eyeing girls, the agent asked softly, "Satisfied?"

"Of course."

"So tell me, please, what all the mystery's about."

Apple said, "What do you know of the present situation here?"

"I read the papers. The Reds are upstaging the West with their double-jointed dancers and their mind-reading magic. London's rife with intrigue. I could smell it as soon as I landed. It's the *why* I don't get."

Apple felt powerful. He forgave the man his put-down, if that's what it had been. Taking two long, loose steps away, he lit a cigarette as if trying to see how slowly it could be done. He strolled around to stand at the man's rear. He told himself he was doing marvellously.

"The double show will be here for two more days," he said. "After a break they appear in Edinburgh for one night, then finish the tour with a performance in Dublin."

"But in different theatres."

"Of course. Wisely, though, the KGB's keeping the whole lot as close together as possible, town by town."

"The ESP thing," the agent said. "That must be making the most real, basic impact, if not with the general public. Any idiot can dance. A bear can dance. But ESP?"

"I believe the Mayflowers are livid."

"No doubt. They think Duke had the last word."

Apple didn't understand the reference. He said, "Naturally."

"But these shows could be so much camouflage," the agent said in the same low tone. "A pair of red herrings. No pun. They wouldn't attract hundreds of foreign spooks."

Apple again felt powerful, the owner of knowledge. "No camouflage. The mind-reading thing, that's to save face for their lag in the space race."

"The Soviet Folk Dancers?"

"They're here for the Kremlin to say, in effect, We don't think this psychic stuff is so great, it's just an everyday thing to us."

The agent said, "They claim to have a telekinesis expert over there who can separate an egg into white and yolk just by looking at it."

"I know," Apple lied.

"Okay, so there's no camouflage. What's the big interest?"

After waiting for an umbrella-swinging man to go by, Apple said, gazing up at the white-streaked figure atop the column, "The word is out on defection. One of these hundred-odd performers is going to skip to the West."

"Word?"

"A rumour that comes on velvet. A rich one. It has to be for so many spooks to be haunting the scene."

The operative put away pen and newspaper. He asked, "Why don't the Reds pack their panties and go home? Right now?"

"The tour's nearly over. All this beautiful face would go to waste if they ran away."

"A far bigger waste if they lost one of the loyal pack. I still have a liking for camouflage."

Apple looked down. "There's nothing else."

"All right," the man said, "a defector." He drew a hand over his brow. "Go on."

"He's scared, apparently. He wants help to escape the curtain rings."

"For Christ's sake. The KGBs can't possibly keep an eye on everyone in that bunch, even if they matched them one for one, and that's ridiculous."

"My man from Upstairs tells me there're seventy-four known Red agents on the loose here, both Hammers and

Sickles. But most are watching us watching them watching the others."

"So there you are. The defector takes a walk and doesn't come back. Couldn't be simpler."

Apple dropped his cigarette and stepped it out. During the act he glanced around. There was no one near except the nuns and girls, who were busy with the pigeons, feeding them and fending them off.

He said quietly, "The majority of the hundred are safe. You couldn't pay them to skip. The apron-string routine. Reprisal against family who're firmly behind the curtain."

"I know, I know," the man said, sounding irritated. He put a hand to the side of his neck. "I feel rotten."

"What?"

"Nothing. Go on."

"For another thing," Apple said, "no one's going to care much if a lowly wardrobe-mistress changes sides."

"It'd still be a face-drop. And because of that the Israelis might snatch someone and claim defection. The cheeky bastards."

"Would they do that?"

"Did Eichmann swim to Israel from South America?"

"Ah," Apple said. He noticed that the man seemed to be swaying slightly. He thought he might have been drinking, which wouldn't break any traditions. He said:

"The conclusion Upstairs is that there are maybe twenty that the would-be defector is among, that the KGBs are watching particularly."

"So we have no lead on who?"

"Not from what I've been told."

"Old Angus doesn't give much, does he?" the agent said. When Apple didn't answer he went on, "All we have to do is note which of the hundred aren't allowed out for walkies."

"Not one of them goes anywhere alone. Didn't even before we got the word. That's tight. Final."

The man swayed. He still had one hand to his neck. The other hand he pressed to his brow. "Listen," he said. "I feel awful. Bloody awful." His voice was husky. The words were badly formed, as if he had a mouthful of food. "I'll have to go."

"Go?" Apple asked, alarmed. "Where?"

"Bed. Hospital. I don't know." Turning, he began to walk away. He tottered.

Apple moved quickly level with him. He said worriedly, "You have to be at Batewell Hall. I've got a ticket here for you."

"Too bad. Throw it away."

"I can't do that."

"I've had it. I'm sick." Suddenly he laughed, though with little humour. "This is a great way to have a week in the country."

"What's wrong with you?"

"Christ knows."

"I haven't finished with your instructions yet."

"Sorry," the man said. He and Apple, separated by two yards, continued moving side by side toward the edge of the square. The agent had lowered his hands, which he was holding out for balance. He swayed constantly out of a straight line. His face looked sleepy.

Helplessly, Apple said, "I don't know what to do."

"Do whatever you want, but stop pacing me. Take off."

Apple slowed. "You'll be all right?"

"If I live," the man said thickly. He went weaving on, head down. Two women got nervously out of his way.

Apple came to a slow, reluctant halt. He watched the agent reach the kerb, lean against a lamp-post and start waving an arm at cabs passing in the steady, broad flow of traffic. He looked drunk. But Apple was sure that alcohol didn't have a delayed action.

A taxi pulled to the side. One minute later it had gone from view, taking the agent with it.

Leaving Trafalgar Square, Apple walked slowly up Charing Cross Road. He was bewildered, which annoyed him, for he should have been full of purpose, making snap decisions and clever moves. But, like a kid with a hurt who runs home, all he could think of to do was call in.

Why hadn't he taken another cab and followed?—the peak-time traffic was so slow, he could even have kept close by jogging. Why hadn't he shoved the ticket in the man's pocket?—he may recover in time. Why . . . ?

Clinging with fingertips to his spy rôle, Apple had ignored the first telephone box he came to. He went in another one now, holding the door open with his foot because super-small spaces gave him claustrophobia. He fed coins in the slot and dialled.

A male voice answered with a casual, "Yes?"

Apple said, "I'd like to speak with Mrs. Thunresdag, please." Today was Thursday. A lot of Anglo-Saxon was in current use, polite and otherwise.

"I think you've made a mistake. What number did you dial?"

Apple quoted six digits. The first three belonged to himself, the others identified the person he wanted to talk to. After a long pause the voice said, "Yes, you made a mistake." The line went dead.

So Angus Watkin wasn't available, Apple thought as he

left the booth. No advice from Dad. And soon it would be
time for Batewell Hall.

Apple paused in the act of getting out cigarettes. The
situation hit him. His jaw sagged.

This was it. This was what had constituted one of his
daydreams over the years. It had actually happened. He
was the understudy who takes over when the star gets
sick; takes over and makes a smash success of the part; is
started on his way to the top. This was definitely it.

Apple smiled anxiously. He stood staring into disbelief.
He wasn't aware of lighting a cigarette and throwing it
away after one draw, or of clasping his hands and nodding as he digested, gradually accepted, finally exulted.

Grinning, Apple swung around and set off at a long-
stride walk. He felt as light as a leaf in the wind. His rôle
was forgotten, but only for the moment; the cloak bil-
lowed at a distance, the dagger floated within reach.

Okay, he told himself, we go to Batewell Hall. We take
the agent's part. We have made a snap, pragmatic decision. We can't be penalised for taking things into our own
hands because we did try to ask for direction. The call
was on record.

Apple cornered Trafalgar Square and went onto the
Strand. After looking at his watch, seeing he had time to
spare, he slowed to match the pace of the other pedestrians. The evening panic to leave the city was easing.

Apple made himself be calm and full of purpose. He
thought over the rest of the assignment instructions,
which were now his own. At the hall he was to take his
seat (it was near the front) and watch the proceedings
with a patent mixture of interest and bafflement. When
the Russians had their turn, he was to observe the performance with particular, though covert, care.

There were six people in the team that was the envy of the psychic West. They were said to be average types. Jointly, working on the same mental wavelength, the six read the minds of subjects unknown to them, picking up messages or symbols or pictures.

At any rate, the Russians claimed that the results—near perfect—were the product of mind-reading. It could be, Apple knew, a sophisticated version of the old music hall routine. But that, true or phony, wasn't important. The whole performance was unimportant.

Apple's job was: A, to commit the six to memory; B, to look for signs of what Watkin had termed escape-desire; C, to try to establish, then or later, some sort of rapport.

B, at first sight, was absurd, Apple mused. Was one of the team expected to make signals over the footlights? However: if this short period, maybe thirty minutes, was the only daily exposure of the six to the public, then it was just possible that the hopeful defector would attempt to get his call for help across to someone watching, via an attitude, a sign, a cast of feature.

Apple presumed that the more direct methods of approach to the six had been tried by Intelligence, using plants such as chambermaids, drivers, clerks. Those methods must have failed.

Apple also presumed that he was not the only operative on this assignment—either foe or friend. Angus Watkin wasn't above giving his people competition from their own side.

Apple realised that he was striding again. He went on doing so. Soon he had passed the Aldwych crescent. He glanced up, as he had often done before, to the crags above the Royal Courts of Justice. There stood Moses,

Christ and King Alfred. Apple wondered how a cake-
burner had got in with those other two.

Which, as he turned into Chancery Lane, he put aside
for a less trivial question: Face apart, was it reasonable
for so many countries to be so vitally interested in a single, unknown defector?

Batewell Hall, a grim building, was one hundred years
old. For lectures, meetings, slide-shows and other as-
semblies, it had been hired traditionally by the more se-
date of England's organisations. Trouble-makers such as
politics and religion were discouraged. Batewell Hall's intentions were serious.

Entering the lobby, after showing his ticket at the door,
Apple found himself among a crowd of people who were
conservative and even drab. He felt visually at home.

Less so were the three Hammers and a Sickle standing
by the doors to the auditorium. Tailoring was enough of a
give-away: those upholstered, heavy, glum suits so popular with Eastern Europeans. The four were squat, barrel-
like, and the Sickle's breasts gave her still more bulk,
though that and the long skirt were all that set her apart
as a female. All had short curly hair and broad flat faces,
hard eyes and gorilla noses.

One of the men was the obvious leader. He had a smile.
In his world, as Apple was aware, you needed the
confidence of authority to appear friendly among Westerners. His top teeth were silver, a common feature of
Iron Curtain dentistry. He had a large grey wart under
one eye.

Apple chose the leader's door as he drifted along with
the crowd. Smiling pleasantly, looking alert and baffled,

he passed by the man with the wart and gave him a nod.
He got one in return, brief and disinterested.

Apple found his seat, sat down, glanced around. He
was on the second row, by the aisle. The stage was bare
except for upright chairs. The backdrop said International
Parapsychological Congress, underscored by the flags of
participating countries.

Soon the five-hundred-strong audience was present and
settled. The last to sit before the lights dimmed, at the
end of a front row, was the man with the silver teeth.

A woman came from the wings to polite applause. She
was English and shy. Mumblingly she talked about Aims
and Mutual Trust. She was followed by a man who read a
paper on poltergeistism. Apple understood a good third of
it.

Two other speakers had a turn before the Russian dele-
gation was announced. The audience rustled with antici-
pation. Apple noted that Silver-teeth eased around to sit
semi-sideways.

Strong applause rose as from the wings came seven
people, three of them women. Six sat on chairs after placing them close together; a huddle, not a line. The seventh,
female, came to the footlights.

She looked to be in her late twenties. Her plump body
strained a trouser suit that was several years out of fashion. She wore blue-tinted spectacles and her hair waved
forward around her cheeks.

The clapping died away. In correct but stilted English,
the spokeswoman talked about the advanced experiments
that were going on in the Union of Soviet Socialist Republics. They would lead to a greater understanding of
mankind, she said, and could only help maintain the bal-

ance of peace, unlike certain other tests that were taking
place around the world.

It was a subtle speech. It had been written by an expert. The slap it gave on the West's wrist was avuncular.

The woman next talked of extra-sensory perception.
She made it sound simple, the baby of all experiments.
The suggestion here was that although other countries,
surely, had also perfected this psychic stage, Russia was
happy to be open about her progress.

"I would like now," the woman said, "to call upon a
member of the audience to act as a volunteer."

A man got up promptly. He went to the steps at one
side of the stage. His manner was determined, his face
stern. He shook hands with the spokeswoman, who then
asked him to identify himself. He gave a name, an address, and said he was a bank manager.

The woman led him to a chair that she had placed on a
level with the team. He sat. She stood at his side. She
said:

"I ask this gentleman to please create in his mind a picture. Any kind he desires, though it should have at least
one strong feature. Continue, please."

The man closed his eyes. The team stared at him intently, leaning forward. Apple looked at the team.

He had done so several times while the spokeswoman
had been making her artful propaganda. Some of the six
he had already fixed in his mind. As he had been told,
they were average types. Their ages ranged from twenty-
five (a girl) to sixty (a man with a white moustache).
They were unremarkable. They might have been sitting
in the waiting room of a suburban doctor.

Apple memorised faces and forms, using tricks he had
been taught in Training Five. His attention he settled on

the girl, because she was pretty. In her case, the mnemonic he used was a correlation between her ankles and the bridge of her nose; they had a similar line. All he would need to do in future was think nose-ankles and the whole figure would spring to his mind.

The team leaned back, exchanged glances, whispered together. The older man stood up and said in Russian, "It's a picture of a field with three white buildings in it."

The spokeswoman translated into English. The volunteer said, "Yes, that's it exactly."

Apple joined in the applause, and again when the team described the next, more complex thought-picture created by the man, who was no longer looking stern. Apple stopped considering the possibility of fraud. He had no need to act bafflement.

After the man's third and last transmission, he shook hands humbly with each of the six before leaving the stage. The spokeswoman said, "Could we have another volunteer, please?"

Apple found himself getting up.

"You're cautious, Porter," the don said, pouring himself more tea. "You're still pretending you don't know what I'm talking about."

Apple looked out of the window of the professor's room. He thought he could never tire of the view: trees and ivy-beaten walls against a background of Gothic spires. He said:

"I want to be sure I understand, sir."

"Of course. And don't get me wrong. I think your caution is admirable. How's the cake?"

"Marvellous, thank you," Apple said. He turned back to the old man. "I suppose I ought to tell you, sir, that

I've been through a similar conversation to this already, a few days ago."

The don smiled. "I know. It was inevitable, with your gift for languages. Atwater couldn't resist. Especially since you attended that reception last week for the *Daily Worker* editor."

"You seem to know a lot about my movements, sir."

"We do, don't we?" the old man said, still smiling. "We also know, or think we know, that your slight Socialism is strictly of the British persuasion."

"That's true."

"But you didn't say as much to Professor Atwater?"

"I said nothing, actually. It was cat-and-mouse."

The don sipped his tea before continuing. "If, now or later, you have ideas of a career in the service of your country, and let us assume for simplicity's sake that you have, then it would be best to decide now how risky you want said career to be."

Apple shook his head. "This time I really don't understand."

"Respected colleague Atwater," the don said gently, "is a rival of mine. He recruits for the other side. He is blissfully unaware that we know of his Communism and his work. At least, we hope he is."

"Does he know of your work, sir?"

"Oh yes. Has for years. We thought it would make him feel more secure if we gradually let him in on my little extra-curricular game." The old man laughed. "He even sends me likely prospects."

"Isn't that dangerous?"

"We reject them nicely."

"I see," Apple said. "I also see why you asked me here today, when Professor Atwater's in London."

"Quite so. And the reason I invited you at all, rather than waiting till end of term, as planned—we've had an eye on you too—is because of Atwater making his move a few days ago. Because, in fine, of the risk."

"I'm afraid I'm being rather dense, sir."

"Not at all," the old man said. "I'm being obscure. I enjoy it. It adds flavour to this sedentary position I play in the game."

Apple asked, "Is that what espionage is, sir, a game?"

"To most of those in it, yes. If they're serious. Anyone who tells you, for analogous instance, that policemen hate criminals, is out of his mind."

"That I do understand."

"Good," the don said. He popped a piece of cake in his mouth and chewed with relish. "But to risk. Are you a brave man, Porter?"

"In a word, no."

"Which means you probably are, but that a natural caution would keep you from situations that might create the opportunity to find out."

Apple smiled. "I'll tell myself that the next time I'm in need of an ego boost."

The don said, "Bravery might never be called for, but it's best to consider the possibility."

"Of course."

"And the possibility is stronger if you take the Atwater way instead of mine. The simple is safe. Still in the dark?"

Apple said, "No, I think I'm beginning to see."

"Tell me what you see, Porter."

"Professor Atwater recruits agents. They would work in this country for Russia. Some, undoubtedly, would be genuine, but known to you, so relatively harmless. Most, since you're often in it from the beginning, would actually be working for you. They would be double agents. If I got involved with Atwater, I too would become a double, with all the accompanying risks."

"In a nutshell, my boy. And does the doubling notion appeal to you?"

Apple shook his head. "I don't like the thought of having a split personality. If I joined the game, it would have to be on a straight basis, play on one side only."

"Do you think you might join?"

"It's worth turning over in my mind, sir."

"Have some more cake, Porter."

"Thank you."

Eight years later, Atwater and the don were still at the university, recruiting agents, and Apple was still being cautious.

But he was determined to stay in this particular innings, if he possibly could. Which meant he had to ignore his reticence and opt for boldness.

Apple moved to the front of Batewell Hall. Being as he was the centre of attention, he would probably have blushed, except for the fact that he could see another volunteer coming down the side aisle. Apple went into a fast stride.

He won. Passing Silver-teeth, who looked at him now with less disinterest, Apple went up the steps and over to the spokeswoman. They shook hands. Her grip was like a robot's and she gave two efficient up-down jerks.

"How do you do," she said. "Would you care to tell all of us your name, address and occupation?"

Loudly, Apple said, "Appleton Porter, 12 Harlequin Mansions, Bloomsbury. I'm a philologist."

"Thank you. Occupy the chair, please."

Apple sat. He nodded when asked, "You know what is required?" Told to please proceed, he lowered his eyelids to a slit of vision. Through it he looked at the six members of the team. They were leaning forward, faces expectant.

Apple felt the woman's hand touch his shoulder encouragingly. He began to think, over and over, *I know the way to freedom.* The language he used was Russian.

Many seconds passed. The faces of the team stayed the same. Apple thought his phrase slowly and heavily.

The spokeswoman lifted her hand, made a signal. The six conferred. They shook their heads at each other. The leader looked around to say, "Sorry, we couldn't get anything at all."

After translating that for the audience, the woman said, "Would you care to try again, sir? Perhaps with a less complex picture."

Apple wasn't too discouraged. If the would-be defector was in this bunch, he would keep the message to himself rather than share it. Apple had at least made his own position clear.

He closed his eyes and formed a mental scene. Being a man of little imagination, he drew the entrance hall of the block of flats he lived in, looking toward the big front door from the direction of the staircase. Slyly, he had the door standing open.

Apple opened his eyes when he felt the woman's hand move away from his shoulder. The team put their heads together, the leader smiled and said, "A long room with a large door and a table in the middle with letters on it."

The spokeswoman translated while looking enquiringly down at Apple. He said, in truth, "Yes, that's very accurate."

The audience clapped. The sound seemed to hold a

hint of relief. This was echoed in the attitudes of the ESP team. It made Apple try for failure when in a moment the woman's hand urged him on.

He conjured up shots of every wallpaper pattern he could remember, added his tartan robe, a flock of pigeons and his favourite television commercial for detergent. He had gone back to wallpaper by the time the hand left to signal enough.

After huddling with his team-mates, the moustached leader said, "Sorry, all we could pick up was flashes of colour."

The spokeswoman interpreted and told the audience, "The gentleman is perhaps not relaxed enough at the moment to make a good subject."

To token applause Apple got up and went to the steps. In passing in front of the man with the silver teeth, he gave a sad little shrug.

He returned to his seat, hesitated, went on up the aisle. A third volunteer was naming himself as Apple went out into the deserted lobby. He lit a cigarette. Smoking, he started to pace.

He didn't know what, if anything, he had accomplished; didn't know if his message re freedom had been received but ignored; didn't know what his next move should be, or if he was supposed to call it a night and go home.

Apple did know, because of the entrance hall description, that the mind-reading had to be genuine. He had accepted the accuracy at the time with insouciance. Now he marvelled at it. There was no way it could have been fraudulently obtained.

Apple stopped walking. So, he thought, the message *must* have got through. If not to all six, at least to one or more who then worked at garbling it for the others. A garbler could well be one who suspected a team-mate of having defection in mind. But say the message got through to them all. They could only have played at non-reception for three reasons:

A, the phrase was ideologically offensive to good Communists. B, this had been tried on the team already and they were saying, in effect, You've got the wrong people— same if it hadn't yet been tried. C, they were afraid because of Silver-teeth and friends, their KGB watchdogs.

Apple began to pace again. He smoked furiously. Cigarette grown small, he lit another from the stub. He couldn't recall ever having done that before.

Apple decided that the assumed failure had to be a good sign, a hot tip. Had they publicly given him back his message, that would have been a clear forget-it.

Apple threw his cigarette into a sandbox and went to one of the auditorium doors. He peeked through. The Russians had gone from the stage. A man there was reading a paper on apparitions.

Quickly Apple went out of the lobby to the street. Darkness had fallen. He walked to the right. There were no breaks in the facade of the buildings. Turning, he went back, passed Batewell Hall, saw with an easing of his tension the mouth of an alley. He entered it.

Fifty dim yards brought him to a door that was lit by a blue bulb. A sign said Stage Door No Admittance. He tried the handle. There was no give. Even if there had been, he had no idea what he would have done. He was playing the game by instinct, like a boxer out on his feet.

Listening close to the door told him nothing. He moved back along the alley and stood in a patch of shadow to wait.

Fifteen minutes later, the door opened. It released a burst of cheerful human sound. The Russians were coming, Apple knew. Russians love noise.

First out were two Hammers and the man with the silver teeth. Next came the ESP team plus spokeswoman. Close behind were the Sickle and two more Hammers.

The ratio of guards to guarded, Apple noted with encouragement, was almost one to one. Nor did he miss that the KGB weren't contributing greatly to the talk and laughter.

He stepped forward and said in Russian, "Excuse me."

The group came to an abrupt halt. The end of talk was less sudden. It dwindled off as if too good to let go. Everyone stared with interest at Apple.

He said, "On behalf of the United Kingdom Philological Institute, I bid you welcome to Great Britain."

One of the ESP team's two female members giggled. She was matronly and a head taller than anyone else. The leader bowed. Another man said, "How well you speak Russian." Others added an appreciative murmur.

"Thank you," Apple said. "Allow me to introduce myself."

"But you already did, Mr. Porter."

The speaker was Silver-teeth. He moved slightly forward from the rest: the frankly smiling team and their glum guards: the sandwich of pleasantness between crusts.

"I suppose I did, in a way," Apple said. "Impersonally."

The man brushed a thumbnail over his wart. "I'm called Kutuzov. I am Second Secretary to the Cultural Attaché at our embassy here."

Sure you are, Apple thought. Culture's stamped all over you. With hob-nail boots.

Apple was pleased to realise that he was reasonably calm. The prickle of a blush he had felt when the group had first looked at him, that was gone. He would probably feel marvellous, he thought, if only he knew what he was doing.

"Am I to understand," Kutuzov said blandly, "that you are here as a representative of your institute?"

It was an opening. Apple was tempted. But he would have nothing and no one behind him. His superiors would issue a denial. He needed, he hoped, a long-term thing.

Which came to him now in a click of inspiration as, looking from one to another of the group, his gaze rested on the youngest member. Cause might have been born in his surprise that she was prettier than he had realised earlier.

"Well," Apple said, "I'll tell you."

She had a round face and a pointed chin. Her small mouth had a trace of lipstick. The severity of her hair, drawn back flatly into a bun, aided the prettiness. Further aid would have come from a plucking job on the dense eyebrows.

"Because if this is official," Kutuzov was saying, "I'm afraid I must ask you to make your approach through the proper channels. Now, Mr. Porter, if you will excuse us."

"It isn't official," Apple said. "I'm here on my own behalf. I'm here to see the young lady." He bowed toward the girl.

She looked blank. A man told her, "He means you, Olga."

Kutuzov turned back from looking behind. Coldly he

ordered, "You will be good enough to explain, Mr. Porter."

Apple said, "Gladly. I'm here because the young lady is so attractive."

The group exchanged glances, some mystified, some amused. The KGBs emitted quiet hostility. The man with the silver teeth echoed, "Attractive?"

Apple nodded. The girl appeared to be bemused. Her large colleague giggled and said with a strong Leningrad accent, "Her name's Olga Goliski." The Sickle at the rear gave a furious hiss.

Apple said, "I understand this isn't the custom in the Soviet Union, but here it's quite normal. A man is taken by a particular performer in a theatre, and afterwards goes backstage to pay his respects."

There was silence. Apple added, "They call them stage-door Johnnies."

"That," Kutuzov said, "is most interesting. And now that you have paid your respects . . ."

Apple cut in, "I also wish to apologise. It's my fault that the team only scored two out of three when reading my mind. I was busy looking at Miss Goliski, you see. I couldn't concentrate properly. I'm very sorry."

The team spokeswoman adjusted her blue-tinted spectacles. "Thank you. No great harm done. Good night."

"Yes," Kutuzov said, moving forward. "Good night, Mr. Porter."

Apple was forced to step aside. The group went on by. He was given nods and grins by the middle section. The large girl winked. Olga glanced up at him shyly, a trace of a smile at the corners of her small mouth.

Last past was the Sickle. She stopped and turned. While the rest walked on along the alley she asked, her face strange in a try at expressing friendliness, "Where did you learn to speak our language so well?"

"At home," Apple said impatiently. "Books, records, some private lessons."

"I congratulate you, Mr. Porter. Russian is the most complex and extensive of tongues, the richest in vocabulary."

He let that one go, asking, "Is Olga married?"

"No," the Sickle said. "You must have spent many years on the project."

He recognised that she was running interference, a rearguard action. He said, drawing away, "Yes, but my love of all things Russian kept me at it."

The group had gone from sight. There came the sound of car doors being opened. The Sickle said, "Good night." She walked on briskly. Apple followed.

When he reached the street he saw three large black cars. Most of the group had already got in. The rest did so, including the Sickle. Doors slammed, the cars drove away.

"Well," Apple said. He had, first, a sense of let-down that the encounter had ended so quickly. But then he began to lift as he realised how well he had done. Rapport had been firmly established, he might have got his mission across via the message, he had let it be known where he could be contacted. That wasn't bad going for a semi-beginner.

Apple treated himself to a cigarette. It tasted good. He wondered if Olga smoked. He supposed, casually, that he cut a mysterious figure, standing here on the kerb smoking.

Cigarette finished, Apple considered his next move. There seemed to be no point in going back into Batewell

Hall. He couldn't follow the group because he didn't know where they'd gone. If he called Watkin he might be told to bow out. So he would let things hang, go home. But, to milk the occasion, he would go on foot.

Apple set off walking.

The street was long, straight and wide. A perspective of lamps showed stores and commercial premises, all closed. Traffic was as sparse as were pedestrians.

Apple walked at a slow pace. He was still in his rôle. It gave satisfaction, even though he underplayed. Whenever he glanced around to see if he was being tailed, which his non-rôle self knew was highly improbable, he did so with a touch of natural-like awkwardness.

Apple thought back over the stage-door scene, taking it from the moment when the group had halted on seeing him there. He re-ran it slowly. He wanted to see if he could catch any kind of signal that he might have missed before.

At traffic lights that were blinking on amber, he looked behind. The street was as before: a few cars, a dozen walkers in singles and pairs, a taxi crawling in search of trade.

Apple went on. He was still not finished with his scene when it occurred to him that something had been odd about that crawling taxi. He glanced back. The oddity was plain. The for-hire sign was unlit.

He stopped to watch, thinking it could just be possible that he had been followed from the hall.

But by whom?—he mused. The would-be defector, having given the guards the slip? A foreign agent who had seen his performance and hoped he might be on to something? The KGB?

The cab stopped beside a man, who then paused in his walk. The back door opened—so there was a passenger. The pedestrian looked to be talking with the hidden rider. Then the door closed and the taxi crawled on.

Apple went on also. He told himself he was being fanciful. Hopeful, rather. He wanted to be tailed, wanted the innings to stay alive. But there was a mundane answer. The driver and passenger were asking directions.

Apple's smug reply to that was the fact of the Knowledge. Before a London cabbie could get his hire licence, he had to prove he could find any street in the Big Smoke. That was as absolute as the rule that the cab had to be high enough to accommodate a man wearing a top hat.

Apple strode on. Quickly reaching the next main junction, he turned off onto another road. The direction was still roughly that of Bloomsbury. He let five minutes pass before stopping to look in a shop window.

The taxi was there. It had been creeping along in the gutter. Now it swooped over to the other side of the road and halted beside a lone walker. The act of before was repeated.

Puzzled, Apple continued on his way. He thought dully that it could be his own side that were doing the tailing, if that's what it was. The cab could be Ethel. But wouldn't her use be self-defeating?

From local pimps to international spies, everyone knew about Ethel. The old cab had been in government service for thirty years. She had done duty with the Vice Squad, Narcotics and Customs, before passing to the Intelligence departments. It was said that one time a group of NATO operatives had a bet as to who could locate Ethel first. A Canadian won, in two and a half hours, and scratched his initials near the radiator.

Apple cheered on realising that if he was being kept an eye on by Upstairs, it must mean he had tickled something to life. Or, as he had considered earlier, he was being tested with future work in mind.

Rather than change direction again to make sure about the tailing, Apple decided on Method 2: *Stand still and see if he treads water.*

The others were: *Faint and see if he comes to help; Point toward him while asking a policeman the name of that church; Approach directly and say, "Are you following me?"*

Apple strode on until he came to a pub. He went in without looking back. The bar was noisy and crowded, the air chokey with smoke, the clientele mostly young and uncombed. Apple was as inconspicuous as a wrestler in a tutu.

Ignoring belligerent stares, he worked his way to the counter, where he ordered a beer because he thought that the most suitable. He didn't like beer. It gave him hiccoughs. His favourite drink was sherry on the rocks.

Served, he remembered in time that you didn't tip in four-ale bars, paid the exact amount, lifted his glass and turned to face the door.

He sipped the beer. No one came in, though he noticed that several customers slipped out, their attitude toward him seeming to say Copper. He allowed his knees to sag slightly.

After fifteen minutes the only newcomer had been an old woman. She was selling home-made meat pies. Apple felt obliged to buy one. He unobtrusively let it slip to the floor before leaving. He hadn't finished his beer. Hiccoughs he didn't need.

Outside he stood to gaze around, a perfectly natural

act. He was pleased to see that the taxi was still in distant attendance. He turned the other way and set off walking.

Almost at once he heard the growing sound of a motor. He didn't look behind. The sound grew, the taxi came abreast, it pulled into the side and stopped. The back door opened. A woman looked out and said, "Hold on there."

Apple halted. "Are you talking to me?"

"Course I am. There's no one else around, is there?"

"Well, no." He looked at the cab carefully. It wasn't Ethel.

"There you are then," the woman said. She was blond, about twenty-two, dressed flashily and wearing heavy cosmetics. Even from six feet away Apple could smell the perfume.

He looked at the driver, an older man who had his gaze rigidly ahead. Apple asked the woman, "What is it?"

"As if you didn't know," she said, winking.

Apple sighed. After all that, he thought with disappointment. A prostitute. The old jab-in-a-cab routine that was supposed to have gone out of style along with blackout curtains.

"I'll give you a special price, dear," the woman said. "A handsome fella like you."

As Apple began to shake his head, a car came rushing up. It jolted to a stop at an angle across the front of the taxi. It was a police car.

There were two uniformed officers in the front, a man in plain clothes behind, which meant the patrol was CID, not Traffic. Dazed by this bizarre development, Apple stood and watched the three men get out. The front pair went to the taxi, one to the driver and one to the girl. The plain-clothes man moved over to the wall, lazily beckoning Apple to follow.

It wasn't until Apple had got close to the average-sized figure in trench coat and slouch hat that he recognised him—and stopped being dazed. He said:

"Hello, sir."

Angus Watkin said, "Good evening, Porter. You nearly spoiled it by going in that pub. But never mind."

"I wanted to know if I had a tail."

"Three, at least. Our lot and two other men. They're hanging around back there somewhere, watching with interest."

Angus Watkin was a bland-faced man aged between fifty and sixty. Across his top lip lay a ridge which told that he had worn a moustache for many years. His eyes were sleepy, with no hint of alertness or intelligence beyond the average. His mouth looked soft, not ruthless. He gave the impression of being a pleasant bore.

Apple asked, "Am I being protected?"

"God, no," Watkin said. His body was motionless, his hands pocketed. "No one's about to stab you in the back, Porter. I'm here to find out what you've been up to."

"I would've called in, sir."

"Of course you would," Angus Watkin said as if he didn't believe it. "But for one thing, I wasn't prepared to wait around all night. For another, the less contact you make with me the better."

"I see," Apple said. He was feeling better by the second. "How's the agent I met in Trafalgar Square?"

"Ill. Some kind of bug." He spoke impatiently. "Let's get on. We have to make this reasonably fast. For the sake of observers, I'm supposed to be a detective who's trying to get you to co-operate."

"In what, sir?"

"In saying that you were solicited by girly there, so she can be charged to that effect."

"She's really one of us, though."

Angus Watkin nodded. "As well as being a genuine whore. Which she has a record to prove. And the driver's a real cabbie."

"As well as being on the team," Apple said. He wondered if these two faceless ones were as pleased as he was with tonight's beckon into brief active service. But was his going to be all that brief?

Risking disapproval, Apple spoke just as his superior was opening his mouth to do the same. He said, "By the way, sir, I know why you used me particularly as a courier tonight."

"Do you really, Porter?"

"Yes, sir. It was so I could tell the agent about matters psychic, should he have any questions. You must have found out about my knowledge of the parapsychological field." By manner and tone he shamelessly implied that he thought the discovery brilliant.

Watkin's face, as usual, gave nothing away. "Quite the expert, are you?"

"Well, a student," Apple said, modest. "At the moment I'm studying telekinesis." He hoped he had the word right. "Did you know they have a woman in Russia who can divide an egg into yolk and white just by using her mind?"

"I do now. But I'd have to see it."

"Well, yes, I would too."

Watkin said, "To the team of mind-readers. Tell me what went on at Batewell Hall."

Concisely, Apple described what had happened before,

during and after the performance. He ended, "I've struck something, obviously."

"Why do you say that, Porter? Why obviously?"

"If I'm being tailed." He spread his hands.

"They could be our friendly foes, for all I know."

Apple blinked; once. He asked himself if they thought him dense as well as too tall, too sympathetic, and a blusher. All this quick action, to mention nothing of the elaborate—the girl, the cab, the police—and Watkin was trying to pass the whole deal off as nothing especially big.

Apple checked his impulse to put that into words. With Watkin you never knew where you stood, and the position he stood in now might not improve if he appeared to be seeing what he shouldn't.

He said, "Surely we'd know if the Mayflowers were against us in this, sir."

"I do wish people wouldn't use slang," Angus Watkin said, though he betrayed no aggravation. "And as for the Americans, we rarely know what they're up to." He looked beyond Apple. "It wouldn't hurt, Porter, if you made a few negative gestures."

Apple acted some shoulder-moving and head-shaking. He went as if to leave, came back, shook his head again. Angus Watkin nodded to signal sufficient.

"The team tonight," Apple said. "The girl I mentioned, Olga Goliski, she was definitely trying to get something across to me out there in the alley."

"Is that right?"

Apple nodded, lying on with, "I feel sure she picked up my message about the way to freedom."

Watkin said, "That would be a nice coincidence."

"I beg your pardon?"

Angus Watkin's eyelids seemed to grow heavier. This,

as Apple was aware, meant that the older man was about to enjoy himself. The only time he showed emotion, it was in and around his eyes; because of the observable actions and reactions for which he was responsible, they were his creations.

Body still motionless, he said, "We have come by a piece of information. By barter. I don't suppose for a moment that we got the best end of the deal."

Which was probably the reverse of the truth, Apple thought. He said, "Someone has to lose, sir."

"Quite so, Porter. It all depends on one's bargaining position. We went into a buyer's market. However, what we've traded for is useful."

The two uniformed men left the taxi and went to lounge near the front of the police car. The girl kept her door open.

Watkin said, "Our information is that three of the mind-reading people have weak ties back in Russia. The strong ties, as you know, are children and parents. Spouses seem to be fairly expendable, which is natural enough."

Cynic, Apple thought. He said, being the toady, "Yes, sir."

"These three have no parents living and no children. Two of the three are female."

"Oh."

"Oh indeed, Porter."

Apple said quickly, "Then I was right about Olga trying to get something across. The other one too, the big one, there was a definite rapport with her. She liked me. You know the way Russians are. They either take you to their bosoms at once, or dislike you for the rest of their lives."

"Yes. Odd people."

"The big one, in fact, told me Olga's name." Because that was true, he said it again.

Angus Watkin asked, "Without giving her own?"

"Yes, sir."

"One would almost think there was a message there."

That this hadn't occurred to Apple would normally have irked him. Now he was too stimulated with hope. He forced his hand:

"This is perfect, sir. With the rapport that I've firmly established, with my Russian and with my knowledge of the psychic as a mutual interest, why, I've got more than a head start. The rest should be fairly straightforward."

Watkin looked at him steadily. His eyelids were still swollen. Apple kept his eagerness and worry hidden, wearing an efficient confident smile. He wished, for the millionth time in his life, that he weren't so tall; that he didn't have to look down on the other man.

"Yes," Angus Watkin said blandly. "All right."

"I stay on the assignment?" Apple asked, aware of a high pitch in his voice.

"For the time being. Play it your own way."

"Yes, sir."

"I'll be in touch," Watkin said. "Don't call in unless it's an emergency. Your cover's your best friend. Stay alone and clean." He moved away with a nod toward the cab. "Now go and have intercourse with girly there. Good night."

The police car drove off. Apple watched it until it had gone from sight along the dark street. He told himself he could have heard incorrectly.

Turning at a sound, he saw the girl getting out of the

cab, and knew there was nothing wrong with his hearing. He went to meet her. She said:

"Smooth bastard, isn't he?" Her accent was still Cockney.

"Yes. Sorry if I put you to some extra trouble by going in the pub."

"No bones broke. Just a bit more hanging around. I went back and chatted up a john who'd already turned me down."

"When you were putting on a show to make your approach to me believable?"

She nodded. "If it was." She shook her head. "That Watkin."

Apple wondered if she were less of an operative, more of a submitter—for favours rendered, or reprisals threatened. He thought he'd rather not know.

He asked, "Did you happen to solicit one of my tails?"

"Naturally," she said. "Anything for a giggle, that's me."

"Foreigner?"

"Australian accent. A freelance, I should think. Maybe working for the Chinese."

Apple said, "Or an innocent tourist from Melbourne who's looking for the swills of the East End."

"That could be, sure," the girl said hurriedly.

Apple realised with a lift in ego that he was being treated with deference. The girl, patently, thought him a top-flight pro. She never heard of good old Russet Appleton. He said a kind:

"But you could be right. Australia breeds the world's best con-men, and from there to spooking isn't far."

"No, it isn't," the girl said. "Got a match?"

They lit cigarettes. The driver of the cab sat quiet and patient. A faint sound of singing came from the pub.

Apple felt so good that he stretched upward his six feet seven inches. His ego was nicely round and full, the mission had been left in his care—save for one final instruction.

He asked, "Know what Watkin wants us to do now?"

"Certainly."

"But do you know why?" He inferred that he himself knew but doubted if she did.

The girl blew out a stream of smoke. "Certainly."

Stern, the mentor, Apple said, "Explain it."

Like a child reciting at a party, the girl said, "There's always the chance that Ivan might go the whole hog in seeing if this pick-up was genuine. He could do a background check on the driver and me, and we're twenty-two carat. But if he checked on you or me for evidence of intimacy, and there was none, well, there you are."

"Good. And how would he check on us, please?"

"Follow one or the other of us afterwards and put us out. Chloroform or something."

Although Apple nodded, he was thinking he had never heard of anything so fantastic in his life. Did the various sides really go to such absurd extremes? Sometimes, obviously, but in a case like this?

While squashing out his cigarette underfoot, he asked, "Do you know what this is all about?"

"No, and I don't want to. It's none of my business. Not that you'd tell me the straight story anyway, would you?"

Apple smiled and raised an eyebrow. The girl flicked her cigarette stub away. "I'm ready when you are."

They went to the cab and got in. The driver took it along the street at a smart pace. The girl said, "This'll cost you twenty pounds. If you've got that much on you. If you haven't, you can always borrow it from the cabbie."

"I have enough," Apple said. He told himself there was nothing like being detail perfect.

"Good, cos it'd take him for ever to get it back from Upstairs. You know what they're like. Though I reckon it must be a bit easier for you."

"A bit, yes."

The taxi turned off the main road, turned again into an alley, and came to a stop nose-in at a warehouse door. The cabbie killed motor and lights, got out, strolled away.

"He knows all the best spots," the girl said. "Been at this lark for forty years."

Apple said, "Tell me, what would you have done if one of those men you approached before me had been interested?"

"I'd've asked too much money."

"Of course."

"But when I leave here, I'm me own boss. I'll graft on for an hour or two. I've got a living to make, y'know." She heeled her shoes off. "It might not be as exciting as yours, what I do, but it has its moments. Like this one."

"Yes?" Apple said, looking at her in the dimness.

She fumbled at her waist, rose off the seat and with a single tug whipped off a wrap-around skirt. From the navel down she was naked. It happened so unexpectedly that Apple had to think snowdrift, snowdrift.

The girl came to him. Her voice dropped to a murmur. "Even though it's all for the cause," she said, "we might as well enjoy it."

Apple stopped thinking snowdrift.

TWO

The Bloomsbury flat had a view of a rear corner of the British Museum. Its other advantages were large rooms with high ceilings, central heating and walls thick enough to abnegate neighbour noise. The furnishings were pseudo-Edwardian.

It was an expensive apartment, but Apple could afford the rent because of his undercover retainer in addition to the wage he got from the Institute. The former, for the sake of cover, he explained as coming from private translation jobs, which, in fact, he did sometimes do for import-export firms. Apple had no financial worries.

Even so, the first thing he thought of on waking the next morning was yesterday's expenses. He was going to be thoroughly the pro. But he decided against going all the way. He wouldn't pad.

Lazily getting out of bed, he put on his screaming tartan robe and went to the kitchen to fix coffee. When he had drunk it he came fully awake and looked at his watch. It was eight o'clock. He took more coffee with him into the living room, where he sat at his typewriter to peck out the expense account. Finished, it looked suitably quaint and mysterious:

      Corn for pigeons . . . . 15 pence.
      Bus ride . . . . 18 pence.

Beer .... 30 pence.
Services of prostitute .... 20 pounds.

Leaving the paper in the machine, where he could glance at it occasionally, Apple finished his coffee and searched out the past few days' newspapers. From an article on the visiting ESP team he learned that their hotel was the Oceansea, which was in the same general area as Batewell Hall. The writer noted sardonically that the troupe's lesser beings were billeted in a humble hostel. The article was short; most coverage on the visiting Russians was given to the dancers at the Royal Festival Hall.

After showering, Apple dressed to his usual neatness and made breakfast. He had two boiled eggs followed by toast with lemon marmalade. The eggs he served to himself in a piece of china he normally used only at Christmas and on his birthday: a rare Crown Derby double-headed egg cup. Today was special, and maybe tomorow would be as well.

Dishes washed, Apple telephoned the home of a book collector and dealer. Apple knew he was an early riser. They had been friends ever since Apple had said, apropos of Lytton Strachey, "If he'd written his book in 1837, would he, I wonder, have called it *Imminent Victorians?*"

Greetings over, Apple asked, "Where's the best place to buy works on the occult?"

"The black arts and so forth?"

"I suppose so. I'll have to start at the beginning. It's for a translation. I need the English terminology."

The bibliophile said scornfully, "The best shops in that field are right on your doorstep. In front of the BM. Where are your eyes, boy?"

Apple made a joke about always expecting the Elgin

Marbles to come rolling out and challenge him to a game. He rang off and left the flat, went down three flights of stairs and into the entrance hallway.

From the centre table he collected his mail. It was non-personal—two bills—which was standard, as he was a poor correspondent. There was an oddity, however, in the fact that his letters were out of alphabetical sequence in the mail chain. He hummed and went out to the early morning greyness.

Two minutes later Apple was walking along the street that fronted the British Museum, though across the road from the thick black railings. He realised why he had never noticed what lay beside him here, despite having come this way a thousand times. The squat building opposite had a threatening manner. It needed watching.

What Apple thought about next was the museum's Reading Room, with its eight million titles and Karl Marx sitting there working on his masterpiece, or serfpiece, because of which, over a hundred years later, a man called Porter was being shadowed in the street outside.

At least, Apple had the feeling he was being shadowed. He could no more prove it than he could state definitely that the mail displacement was anything other than accidental. But he hoped for both. It would be a good sign.

Apple found half a dozen shops that appeared to specialise in the supernatural. None of the bookstores being open yet, he browsed at windows, comfortable in the knowledge that under the circumstances of last night's stage-door Johnnie act, he was doing exactly the right thing.

At nine sharp a small thin woman came and opened one of the shops. Apple followed her in. He explained, while choosing three books on various aspects of para-psychology:

"I'd like to learn something about the subject. I've just met someone who's an expert and I want to make a good impression. You know how it is." He admired his subtlety in not saying that the someone was female.

The woman gave him a 5 per cent discount. He set off home, walking briskly, and again made no attempt to ver-ify what his feelings told him about a tail.

In the flat he put through a call to his superior in the Kensington mansion that housed the UK Philological In-stitute. Professor Warden was a frail- and lost-looking man who was fluent in fourteen languages but could never think of the word he wanted in English.

He expressed concern when Apple said he wouldn't be coming in today, he was sick.

"Sorry to hear that, Porter. What are the—er—?"

"Symptoms," Apple said. "Sweating and nausea and a bit of dizziness. I think I've been bitten by a bug. Maybe it's the love-bug."

Professor Warden told him not to treat the matter too lightly, to call a doctor, to take off as much time as he wanted.

After disconnecting, Apple wondered if he was being overcautious in placing that love-bug dart. It was hardly likely that someone would go to the Institute and ask why he wasn't at work. But then, all the details so far had been extreme, even ludicrous. Leaving out the girl and her transportation, there was the police patrol.

That, at first glance, seemed simple. But Apple appreci-ated that it wasn't just a matter of walking into the nearest police station and saying let's go.

Watkin would have to worm through the Home Office

to get at the Special Branch, who looked after counter-
espionage. They would have to be flattered into allowing
contact with Scotland Yard, who, if they were in the
mood, would let the Metropolitan Police help to the extent of supplying officers and men. A complex affair. Even
if the set-up had been phony, car and uniforms from the
Intelligence dressing-room, it was still a lot of trouble.
Too much trouble to justify the end?

Apple shrugged. He picked up the books and looked at
his watch. He would read for one hour.

He hated the hotel on first sight. It was so new he could
pick out splashes of paint on the paving stones. With the
balconies formed in continuous lines, layer upon layer,
the place looked like a giant venetian blind.

The hotel couldn't have been a better choice as a sym-
bol for the Red isolation attitude, Apple thought. We're
looking out at you but you can't look in on us, except
when we want you to.

There was bustle at the front of the hotel. People were
coming or going or standing about, most wearing the
keen-eyed stamp of the tourist. Cars and cabs arrived,
left, dawdled. A doorman in Gilbert and Sullivan finery
was on tip-taking patrol.

Apple crossed to the revolving door, holding promi-
nently his bunch of carnations. Their purchase in the
flower shop had given him a minute of hard thought, the
available colours suddenly taking on deep political
significance. He had finally decided on a selection of red,
pink and white. You had to be careful.

The lobby was crowded and noisy, the reception desk
busy. It was some time before Apple got attended to.
During the wait he derided the seascape decor while

picking out the two Hammers who were pretending to read newspapers.

That made Apple scornful. The reading ploy had been preached against in Training Three: *In a busy place the man who shows no interest in the passing scene is acting a lie.*

"Yes, sir?" the clerk asked.

"I have an appointment to see one of your guests," Apple said firmly, his smile confident. "Miss Olga Goliski."

The clerk opened a book. He repeated the surname as he followed his forefinger down a page. "I don't see it," he said. "Ah yes. Here. The lady's sharing a room."

Apple, quickly: "Is that other lady Alicia Diaghilev?" He forgave himself the cute invention.

"No, sir. Miss Natasha Krupskaya."

"Of course."

The clerk looked up, his face doubtful. "But I've just remembered. I'm afraid there's no question of seeing any of our Russian visitors. They are not to be disturbed under any circumstances. The press can be such a bother."

"I'm not press. I'm Miss Goliski's second cousin."

"Even so. They have their meditating to do. We're not allowed to clean the rooms. They do it themselves."

A voice said in Russian, "Good morning."

Apple looked aside and down. Grossly beside him was the Sickle who had been at Batewell Hall last night. Her expression was cold. Now, at close range and in strong light, Apple saw that she shaved. He was glad.

The clerk excused himself and moved away. Apple said pleasantly, "Good morning, Miss Krupskaya."

"That is not my name."

Which, Apple thought, meant that Olga's room-mate had to be the big girl, a possible ally.

He said, "I'd like to see Olga, please."

"Not allowed," the Sickle said. "The team is exhausted with seeing people."

"Five minutes. To give her these flowers as a small token of my esteem."

"Not even five seconds, Mr. Porter. Good morning." She turned and trundled away.

Apple beckoned to the clerk, who came over with a wary look. Apple gave him the flowers. "Would you please see that these get to Miss Goliski. She's in room—er —room—" He snapped his fingers. "What *was* that number?"

"I'll see that they get delivered," the clerk said. He put the bouquet out of sight and went to another client.

Apple told himself you couldn't score every time. He strolled away from the desk. A paper-reading Hammer now sat near the lifts, the Sickle was on guard by the stairs.

Not, Apple felt sure, that they were the full extent of the barrier. There would be more security upstairs. And if by chance the flowers got that far, they would be shredded and scrutinised.

Apple made for a sign that said Twenty League Coffee Shop. Below it, steps led him down to a mock-up of a submarine interior. Any five-year-old would have been convinced for minutes on end. Fish stared sadly through large portholes. Staff in navy uniform stood behind a self-serve counter.

Apple got a coffee and went to a table shaped like a sailor's hat. For ten minutes he sipped, smoked, watched the tourists, while being unaware of these acts. He was wondering about his next move.

So he didn't see the man come in, which—the manner of entrance—might have told him something. First he knew was a voice saying, "Excuse me. Weren't you on the stage last night at Batewell Hall?"

He was medium build but with a thick neck. He wore a sports shirt and Madras jacket, both in technicolour. About twenty-five, he had a plain face and innocent blue eyes. His accent would have sounded Australian to the unschooled in dialects. Apple knew it for South African.

He nodded. The Capey said, "Thought so. My name's Harry Wall. And yours is Portman."

"Porter."

"Right. Mind if I join you? Thanks." He sat down with his sandwich and a glass of milk, looked around the room and said, "Very clever."

"I suppose it is."

"My first time here."

"And mine."

"Is that a fact?" Harry Wall asked, blinking his blue eyes. "Thought you might be staying here." He smiled. "Tell you the truth, I thought you might be part of the act."

Apple shook his head. "Do you think the mind-reading's phony?"

"It was an idea. I don't know. I don't know a damn thing about all this stuff. But I want to find out. It could be worth a story. Trouble is, though, you can't get to see any of these people."

"I just found that out."

His face candid, Harry Wall explained that he was a writer, non-fiction. He was paying his way on a year's stay in the UK by doing pieces for South African publications, and trying to avoid the hackneyed themes such as the Crown Jewels and Big Ben. This psychic bit was exactly what he was looking for.

"If I could only get an interview with one of the team, Porter, I'd be in like Flynn."

If it was a cover, Apple thought, it wasn't bad as covers went. But the vivid clothing, that was a mistake. He said, "Sorry I can't help you. I need help myself. I've taken a fancy to one of the girls on the team, but she's not allowed to see anyone."

Wall said, "Maybe we should pool our resources."

Apple smiled. "We haven't got any."

"Oh, I don't know," Wall said. He took a sip of milk and pulled a face of disgust. "What time do the bars open?"

"Eleven o'clock," Apple said, adding in thought: As anyone who's been in Britain for more than a few days would surely know.

"Oh well."

"But about resources."

Harry Wall huddled forward over his elbows like a conspirator. "I picked up a whisper the other night. Won't say how. A true writer protects his sources. But this whisper is sound. I'll give it to you if you'll give me something in trade. A lead of some kind, or whatever."

"If I had the ghost of a lead," Apple said, "I wouldn't be sitting here twiddling my thumbs. I ought to be at work." He told about his job.

Harry Wall said, "Not bad."

"Mmm?"

"That job. Must pay nicely."

Apple shrugged. He said, "This trade of yours. How

about if I give you the name of the man in charge of the ESP visitors. The man with the silver teeth."

"I've seen him around. Looks like a spy to me. In fact, *you* could be a spy for all I know." He was smiling again.

Apple laughed. "Silver-teeth's name is Kutuzov. He's a cultural attaché." He added in Russian, "He might talk to you."

The hesitation was brief. Wall said, "What's that?"

"Sorry. I said I don't think he speaks English."

"Okay, then maybe you could translate for me."

"That's an idea," Apple said. He thought that either Wall was what he claimed, or an operator clever enough to play the clown. "What's your whisper?"

"This team of mind-readers," Wall said, still the furtive anarchist. "One of the six is an odd man out. He's not genuine. He doesn't read minds."

"What's he there for?"

"Security, maybe. Could be one of those KBGs or whatever they call 'em."

Apple didn't bother to correct the initials. He was annoyed for not having thought of this himself. If it were so, it would explain why the freedom message hadn't been allowed to be voiced.

He asked, "Which one of the six is it supposed to be?"

"Search me, Porter," Harry Wall said. "But listen. How about this interpreting thing with Kutuzov?"

Apple got up. "Perhaps. If I happen to be around. Or if you can fix it with him."

Wall searched his person hastily, found a card, thrust it into Apple's hand. "You can reach me at that number. I might even cut you in on the fee. We might even split the by-line."

"See you," Apple said.

In the lobby, the Hammer and Sickle were still on guard. Apple gave each a friendly wave as he crossed to the exit, though his mind was on Harry Wall and what his possible game was and if he could be used in some way.

On the street Apple set out to circle the block. He came to a service lane and entered. On either side were gates that led to back yards. The one belonging to the Oceansea Hotel, midway along, was obvious on two counts: the number of garbage cans, the dark-suited man leaning on the gate.

Apple slipped into a yard on that same side. He hadn't been seen by the Hammer, who was reading what looked like a sex magazine, his manner furtive.

The yard was full of junk. Apple used a broken chair to help in scaling the wall. He dropped down into the neighbouring yard, strode across it, and was halted by seeing that the next wall was topped with broken glass. There were still three or four back yards to cover before he got to the hotel's.

Apple thought about it.

He was looking at the premises that owned the yard, wondering if he could find in there something to cover the glass, when he got a better and simpler idea.

He went to the door. It was unlocked. Pushing it open, he went through, into a room where three girls were stitching. They looked at him in surprise.

"No," Apple said, "it won't take long to repair. Carry on, ladies." He went through another, empty room, along a passage and into a dress shop. Present were so many women that he didn't know staff from customers. No one gave him a glance. He was vaguely disappointed.

Outside, Apple told himself that, as he could have gone

around by the lane, taking that interior route had been unnecessary. He was making the most of his innings.

Next door to the hotel was a small department store. Apple went in. He strode out its narrow length, passed through swing doors marked Staff, and collided with a man.

He wore a flower in his lapel: the manager uniform. Recovered from the meeting, he snapped, "Who the hell are you?"

Apple, furious to find himself blushing, though mildly—and, he assured himself, from shock not embarrassment—straightened his jacket and raised a finger to his lips. He whispered, "Not so loud, please."

"What?"

"You go to the front. I'll check the back."

The man stared. "Now, look here."

Apple moved by him and patted his shoulder. "Play it cool, old man. We're relying on you." He went on swiftly, reached a door and drew it open. As he slipped outside he saw the man still standing there. He gave him a solemn nod.

Cartons lay against the wall. Apple climbed with ease. He lowered himself into a yard crammed with bottle-crates and swill-bins. There were two doors, both wide open. One let out kitchen clatter and the stench of frying. The other gave into a vestibule lined with fire extinguishers.

From over the wall came the manager's voice, saying, "He went this way."

Apple strode into the vestibule. He closed the door behind him. For several minutes he stood listening, his senses taut. He heard nothing but faint kitchen noises.

He spent longer than the wait in trying to get one of

the extinguishers from its mooring. Succeeding at last, he put the cannister on his shoulder and went into a corridor.

There were stone steps, going up. Apple climbed. He had no firm plan in mind. He would play it by contingency.

He came to a landing where a glassed-in door led to a floor of the hotel proper. Apple went through. Straggling along the corridor—all its doors open—were hampers of linen and cleaning carts.

From one room came singing. In another a woman was telling in Spanish about her son's teeth. From a third drifted the whine of a vacuum cleaner.

Apple moved to the singer's door. She saw him but went on with her song and dusting, until he said, "What are you lot doing here? I thought our Russians did their own cleaning."

The maid told him, "You got the wrong floor, mate. This is the first, not the fourth."

Apple shook his head at his stupidity and retreated. He went back to the service stairs. They were as quiet and deserted as before. He climbed smoothly to keep the heavy cannister from bouncing on his shoulder.

Cautiously Apple peered through the door to the fourth floor. There was no one to be seen. He went through. There was nothing to be heard. All the doors were closed.

Apple began to walk along close to the wall. At the hallway's end he turned and came back at the other side. From beyond only two of the doors had he heard sounds: a mumble of male voices.

In the centre of the corridor were stairs and a bank of lifts. The latter constantly hummed and clicked and flashed lights. Apple expected the doors to slide back at any moment.

Because it was expected, he didn't think it actually would happen, and so was surprised when it did. He was on his second tour of the corridor, moving away from the elevators.

At the hiss of opening doors he stopped, looked back and quickly shifted the fire extinguisher hidingly to that side. He also concaved his back and sagged at the knees.

One person came from the lift. Apple recognised him as a member of the mind-reading team, a youngish man with a farmer ruddiness. He was carrying a pair of binoculars.

Keeping his face mostly behind the cannister, Apple called in child's Russian, "Room of young ladies, please?"

Not bothering to equal the pidginism, the man said he didn't know the number, it was along that end somewhere, but anyway, the girls were out, he'd just left them up on the roof.

"My thanks."

"It gave me pleasure."

When the man had gone inside a room, Apple returned to the service stairs. The cannister he left there beside the door. He started to climb. Soon he was cursing the fact that he was a smoker. He stopped once to sit and rest. The next time he stopped was on the last landing, which was bright with daylight.

Through the glass Apple had a partial view of the hotel roof, with bushes in tubs, striped umbrellas and wickerwork furniture. There were people sitting and strolling. One of the strollers was the big girl, Natasha.

In the next quarter hour, Apple learned all about frustration and what it can do to the nerves. A dozen times the girl seemed to be looking right at him, though she failed to respond to his waves. And he couldn't risk going out. While there were no Hammers to be seen, there could be some, were sure to be some, beyond the edge of his range of vision.

And that, finally, is where Natasha Krupskaya also went. She and her two colleagues stopped their aimless circling and walked out of sight. Apple kicked the wall.

Which was very sensible and real professional, he told himself. Why didn't he lie down and batter his heels on the floor?

Turning his back on the door, Apple sat on the top step. He got out cigarettes and lit one with grumpy movements. After inhaling smoke deeply, he spat it away as if just discovering that it was his enemy.

Calm came. Apple thought the situation over and decided he had to go out on the roof. He had nothing to fear from the Hammers, he knew, but they would run immediate interference when/if they saw him approaching Olga —or anyone else on the team. Ergo: he needed a disguise.

Because he was tapping his feet as an aid to creative thought, Apple didn't hear the door open. Nor did he hear the two light steps behind him. First he knew of having company was being poked in the spine.

Involuntarily he shot to his feet, went down two steps, turned. Smiling at him was Natasha Krupskaya. She said with suppressed excitement:

"Good morning. I saw you waving. I didn't give the show away, however. I took my friends off and left them around the other side, where Olga is."

"Well done."

"You're here because of her, yes?"

"That's right," Apple said. He pinched the cinder off his cigarette, which he pocketed. "I sneaked in."

"Of course you did. You remind me of my Uncle Lazar. He's tall like you. All my family are tall."

Apple went up the two steps. "That's nice."

"Uncle Lazar's a rogue. You wouldn't believe the things he gets up to. He'll end his days in Siberia, everyone tells him."

Apple noticed that the girl had fine, graceful eyebrows. It was as if the hefty body insisted that at least one part of it had to be delicate.

He began, "Miss Krupskaya . . ."

"Call me Natasha, do. Isn't this fun?"

"In a way, Natasha, yes. But I'd like to talk to Olga. I'd be most grateful if you could bring her in here."

"Without anyone noticing." The girl giggled. "Secretly."

"Do you think she'd want to?"

A heavy nod. "We talked about you last night. I believe she's taken quite a fancy. She kept finding fault with you, which is always a sign."

"Can you get her away from the others?"

"I'm sure I can," Natasha said. "But best for you not to meet here. Someone might use the stairs. Come with me."

Two minutes later they were out on the roof, in a cranny formed by chimney stacks. Being ugly, the place was not likely to be patronised by hotel guests.

Natasha slipped lightly away with a hissed, "Farewell, Appleton." He had told her to use his first name and she pronounced it like a small explosion.

Between stacks Apple could see people passing. One of these, alone, was a Hammer. He was listening to nearby strollers, not with the manner of an official eavesdropper, but as if he wished he could join in the conversation. Apple felt a twinge of pity, against which he then steeled himself, remembering the fatal *Tends to be sympathetic.*

There was the tap of quick footsteps. Next, Olga Goliski appeared. Coming to an abrupt stop, she put her hands behind, smiled shyly and said:

"Good morning, Appleton."

Apple was charmed. It was the first time he had ever liked the sound of his name, in any accent. Also he liked her manner, her prettiness and the summery dress that showed off her slight figure.

He said, "Thank you for coming. I hope you won't get into trouble, if anyone finds out."

She gave an elaborate shrug, elbows going out and shoulders up. "I don't care. There's not much they can do. Anyway, we're only talking. There can't be any harm in that."

"What do you think would happen if you slipped away with me for a walk?"

She smiled. "I don't know."

Apple persisted, "I mean, do you ever feel that it would be nice to go away? Right away?"

Another shrug. "I get plenty of fresh air up here. And the view is delicious. You can see all over the city."

Apple nodded. Then they both spoke at the same time. Olga asked if he had an English cigarette, he asked if she had received his flowers. Laughing, they worked it out. Apple felt like a youth on his first date.

He gave her a cigarette and a light. "Ask for your bouquet. They have no right to keep it from you."

"You're very kind, Appleton," Olga said, involved

with her cigarette, which she held up in two poking
fingers like a ten-year-old behind the barn.

"London's an attractive city, isn't it?" Apple said. "It's
a good place to live." He told himself he was being too
subtle.

"Except for the slums," Olga said. "They must be terrible. I've read about them. Dickens is one of my favourite
authors, you see. After the Russian masters, of course."

"I don't know if we have any slums left. I believe
they've all been demolished."

"Oh no. We're going to see them, when we have the
time." She nodded soberly. "Westerners aren't always
aware of what's going on in their own back yards."

"Charles John Huffam Dickens," Apple said, "died
well over one hundred years ago. Things have changed a
little since then."

Olga shook her head compassionately. "Only a little?"

Before Apple could step on that, three men walked in
on them. The apex of the triangle was the man with silver
teeth. He didn't show them as he said, like a movie vil-
lain:

"So, my friend, we meet again."

Apple smiled. "Yes. Good morning."

Olga smoked on, apparently undisturbed by the inter-
ruption. She craned her head forward to the held-up cigarette, rather than bring it to her mouth.

Kutuzov told her, "Your friends are looking for you,
Comrade Goliski. Please don't keep them waiting."

"Very well," she said; and to Apple, "Good-bye. It was
nice seeing you again. I'll ask for my flowers."

Apple bowed. "Good-bye for now."

Olga left, following her cigarette.

"Mr. Porter," Kutuzov said, wiping a thumbnail over

his wart, "I'm afraid I must ask you to stop bothering that young lady."

"She didn't look bothered to me."

"Russian girls are too polite. They will go to great lengths to hide their true feelings for the sake of others. In the West it's different."

"Oh, not very much," Apple said. "But tell me, how did you know I was here?"

Kutuzov showed his teeth. "How do you know that I did know?"

"Well, I suppose because you didn't look surprised. Somebody must have told you."

"All I was told, Mr. Porter, was that a man of an unfortunate height, carrying a fire extinguisher that should have been somewhere else, had been asking for our young ladies' bedroom."

"I see."

"The extinguisher was found on the stairs. The stairs led to this roof. Elementary, Dr. Holmes."

"Quite."

"There's a smudge of orange paint on your shoulder, by the way."

As he brushed at the place where he had carried the cannister, Apple told himself the solution could be as simple as that. He hoped it was.

"Now, my friend," Kutuzov said, "let us see you safely downstairs."

Led and tailed by a Hammer, they went side by side down the stone steps of the stairwell. The four pairs of shoes made so much noise, the man with silver teeth was obliged to shout.

"What were you and Comrade Goliski talking about?"

"Politics," Apple said.

Kutuzov looked at him sharply. "What kind?"

"She was trying to convert me to Marxism." He added, while the other man laughed, "That must be because she's a Party member."

Neatly swerving: "All Soviet citizens adhere faithfully to our way of life. It's in the blood."

Apple knew of several gory replies to that. Instead, he asked what any innocent philologist would. "Did you have me followed last night from the hall?"

Kutuzov stopped. They all stopped. Shouting the first words, then murmuring the rest, Kutuzov said, "I don't know what . . . you mean by that question."

"I had the feeling I was being followed."

"Why, what happened?"

"Oh, nothing in particular," Apple said. He cleared his throat and looked embarrassed. He also tried to blush. He couldn't. He never could, to order.

They started down again. Kutuzov suggested that Apple had read too many trashy novels, as well as believing the anti-Soviet propaganda that was churned out by the Capitalist press. He went on to plug his theme that the mind-reading team should not be pestered.

Passing across the back yard they went through the gate. The Hammer there, an inch of magazine protruding from his sleeve, looked flustered and worried. Apple steeled himself.

He said cheerily, "Good-bye for the present, Mr. Kutuzov. We'll be meeting again, no doubt." He strode off without waiting for an answer.

Out of the lane he went around to the main street. Across the road from the hotel were a score of idlers. Among them were bored-looking members of the Capitalist press, their shoulders being deformed by camera-straps. There were two girls carrying paper Russian flags. There was a man with a placard which asked that Hungary not be forgotten. There was Harry Wall.

Apple went the other way. He thought he would have an early lunch to celebrate whatever it was his feelings told him he had accomplished—and actually getting to see Olga was surely something of an achievement in itself—while at the same time working on the problem of what should be the next step.

Presently he came to an Indian restaurant. He went in despite its smell. There were few tables occupied. He took one from where he could watch the door; next decided that was too obvious and spy-like; changed to where he was behind a pillar.

From the waitress in a Woolworth sari he ordered lamb curry and a glass of milk. When served, he ate with enthusiasm. The milk had turned the penultimate corner but the curry was delicious. He ordered another.

During the forty minutes that Apple was in the restaurant it gradually filled with customers, though there were none he could relate to himself, without being paranoid.

He paid the bill and strolled back toward the hotel. In spite of having formed no plan of action, which was getting to be standard, he felt warm and fine. He thought he might even condescend to call in and ask for advice, but recalled that Watkin had told him that was for emergency only.

From the distance Apple could see that Harry Wall was still among the loungers across from the hotel. The maybe-writer was laughing with one of the pro-Russian girls. Her friend was talking to the man who didn't want anyone to forget Hungary.

Keeping close to the wall, Apple went as close as he dare without drawing Wall's attention. He couldn't make up his mind about the South African, but intended asking for a check on him.

There was a pub ahead. Apple dared another twenty yards—and made the pub safely. He was hoping for a view of the hotel from a front window.

The mid-day drinking session being at its high point, the pub was crowded. Tables dripped spillage. People were standing two deep along the bar. There was more noise than in a teacherless schoolroom. The windows were of frosted glass.

As Apple stood among the crowd, undecided, the door thunked open and a man came in. He was a reporter. He ambled to a corner table, where he slumped down and exchanged yawns with another man with a camera to nurse.

Apple thought about it.

The idea still wasn't clear when, after he had got himself a sherry with ice, the door thunked again and another newsman entered. This one headed for the bar.

He was in his early twenties, had a straggle of beard to lengthen a plump face, and wore a blue serge suit that was old enough to have passed the shiny stage.

Apple intercepted him. He said hotly, "It's no use you following me in here. I have nothing to tell you. No comment. Just leave me alone."

To get rid of a reporter, grab his arm and say you've got the greatest story he's ever heard. Apple was using that in reverse.

And, it seemed, it wasn't working. He stood sipping his drink and fighting the urge to look around. More in-

trigued than worried, he assured himself that if the ploy
flopped with this man he could easily try it on another.

The fish bit. Apple turned at a tap on his shoulder. The
reporter was there, now holding a pint of beer, whose
presence had made his stance more upright and his face
brighter.

"Damn it all," Apple said. "This is intolerable."

Soothingly, the man said, "Now now, old son, take it
cool. I didn't come in here looking for you."

"Oh no. Of course not. Quite coincidental."

"Something along those lines. Or thirst."

"You'll get nothing out of me," Apple said testily.
"There's no story in it anyway, no matter what you've
been told. I'm not even going to give you my name."

The reporter smiled. "Give you mine, if you like. It's
Jim Donald. *Evening Comet*. At your service."

"No, thank you. The only service I require is to be left
in peace." He swung to face the other way. There was silence from behind. He turned back and asked:

"Just what makes people like you think you have the
right to go poking your noses into the private affairs of
others?"

"Well now, old son, it's a free press."

"You're as bad as the KGB."

Jim Donald was good. He took the hook as if it were a
remark on the weather, although he perhaps went too far
in asking, "Isn't that something to do with the Russians?"

"I'm not saying another word."

The man hummed, raised his glass, drank deeply.

"Not another word," Apple said. "This affair isn't newsworthy in the first place. I'm not going to let you worm it
out of me. As I already said, no comment."

After glancing behind him in both directions, the reporter edged closer. He said quietly, "I think you're right, sir. Perfectly right. Some of these journalists have no morals whatever. Destroy a confidence in the batting of an eye, they would. So do keep your voice down. I'd hate for your story to get into the wrong hands."

Sulkily, Apple said, "It isn't going to get into *any* hands."

"That's the way. What they don't know won't do them any good, and do you no harm. Don't say anything, sir. That is my sincere advice."

"Thank you."

The reporter raised his glass. "Cheers."

"Your health."

They drank and went back to work. Apple gave bits of the story between protesting that there was no story to give, and that he had no comment to make anyway. Jim Donald asked questions before shaking his head and saying, "You don't have to answer that, sir, even if it is off the record."

Apple eked the tale of his love for this sweet Russian girl, the barrier of the guards, his playing sick to get off work at the Institute. He slipped his name in with smooth inadvertence: "She asked if Appleton was a real first name," and, later, "He called me Porter without the Mister, just to be offensive." He mentioned that maybe they thought he was a spy or something.

"These Reds have weird minds," the reporter said, all understanding and satisfaction.

Apple drained his glass, took into his mouth the last bit of ice and crunched it. He said, "As you can see, it's not in the least newsworthy. But I dare say some of these unscrupulous journalists would twist it into something lurid."

"You're dead right, old son."

"But you, Mr. Donald, will respect the confidence, I can tell."

The reporter sneaked a look at the clock above the bar. "At the *Comet*, I can assure you, we have a code of ethics to live and work by."

Apple knew that the yellow-press *Comet*'s code was on the style of: If it's white, paint it grey; if it's grey, paint it black; if it's black, bemoan the growing lack of white in the world.

He said, "I'm pleased to hear that."

"Trust is trust."

"That's very profound." He told himself he was going to blow the whole thing if he didn't watch it.

"What's your next move?" the reporter asked indifferently, as a filler. He was more interested in the beer he began to drink at speed, his Adam's apple jerking.

Apple said, in all honesty, "I haven't a clue."

Jim Donald reached through to the bar with his empty glass, wiped his mouth, said, "Why don't you give the girl a buzz on the blower?"

Apple blinked. Telephoning was so obvious that he hadn't thought of it. "Yes," he said. "Why don't I?"

He found a call-box on a street behind the pub, but the directories had been stolen, so he had to look further. The next booth he came to had books, but he discovered he had no change. Nearby shops were still closed for the lunch break.

Apple was pleased by the setbacks. He didn't like it when things continually ran on a level keel; the law of averages was against you. Also, if he had an observer, which

he suspected, this bumbling would look nicely amateurish.

He stopped a passing woman in nurse's uniform and
got change. Going back to the booth, he wondered if now
the nurse would be considered a possible contact, and
tailed. He hoped so. He liked people to be kept busy.

One foot propping the door open, Apple found the
number and got through to the hotel switchboard. He
asked to speak to Olga Goliski. "Her room's on the fourth
floor."

"In the first place," the receptionist said in a dead tone,
"Miss Goliski is accepting no calls. In the second place,
all our Russians are out."

"Out? Oh, I suppose you mean up on the roof."

"Out. Not in. They've gone sightseeing. The coach left
ten minutes ago."

"Ah yes," Apple said. "The slums."

"They don't have slums in the countryside. That's
where they've gone. This is Rural England day."

Trying for rapport, Apple joshed, "All those stately
homes with ghosts and draughts, eh?"

The tone stayed dead. "I wouldn't know."

Responding in kind, Apple explained that he was the
manager of Batewell Hall. "It's important that I know
what time the visitors will be back at the hotel."

"The coach returns at five sharp."

Which, he thought, leaving the telephone booth, gave
him an unwanted four hours, a stretch in need of filling.
Should he go to the pictures? No, that's not what the
smitten did. They gave chase. If they knew where to
chase to. Which would be simple enough to find out—
travel agencies, coach line offices, the official Tourist
Board department for this area.

Yes, simple, if you had training in such detective work. Philologists did not. So what they did was hire themselves cars and go careening about the countryside.

Walking firmly, Apple hoped he wouldn't have the bad fortune to actually come across the Russian party. It was highly unlikely but not impossible. A breathing space on either side could do nothing but good.

A quarter hour later Apple was showing his credit card in a car-hire office. He congratulated himself on having fitted purpose to stage dressing, though knew it was the mention of stately homes that had given him the idea. What he didn't know for sure was whether he was in search of advice, or merely wanted to show off, to say, in effect, See how well I'm doing?

It was the show-off bit, Apple admitted as he drove away in a suitably noticeable car, a white Opel. An operative who was doing well wouldn't dream of asking for advice.

He headed north-east on a thruway. Regular checks in the rear-view mirror told him nothing in respect of pursuit. He was aware, in any case, that the favoured method of tailing by vehicle was to drive ahead of the spot car.

Until the last, final, ultimate dribble of Greater London suburb had been tediously put behind, Apple thought over Harry Wall's information/invention/red herring/ mistake regarding the team of mind-readers. He had a warm feeling about it.

Stopping at a truckers' cafe, he ordered a cup of tea and asked about tourist coaches. The sleepy-eyed owner said they passed all the time; all the time; just passed; he was going to give the front a new coat of paint.

Apple stopped once more to ask, at a service station, before zipping off into back lanes which became progressively more maze-like. He drove as fast as safety allowed. He drove grinning with enjoyment. He was sorry when he saw the ideal place to park.

Reversing through the gateway and to the far side of the haystack, Apple switched off the motor and got out. The silence was awesome. Nothing disturbed it during the ten minutes he waited there.

He was fairly certain he was not being followed.

If he had had company, Apple thought, it would most likely have been only to the first enquiry stop. He wondered if the company had itself had a tail of two bored men from Special Branch, which for years had suffered through embassy picnics and rambles.

Apple got in the car and, regretfully, left the peaceful place. He told himself he must try to get out in the wilds more often. It would be fine to stroll, breathe clean air, lounge around on grass.

Twenty minutes of fast driving along lane and highway brought him to a track, which led to a disused quarry. He left the car there, in among the cottage-size boulders. Out in the open he set off walking.

He had two miles to cover cross-country to reach his goal, which he would have been at by now, had he driven straight there. But he preferred to play the innings on pure defence; play with the idea of staying in the game. On the thousand-to-one chance of him still having a tail, or an electronic tracer on the car, or some other scientific miracle unknown to him, he would not be blowing his cover by leading the way to Damian House, whose true character could well be known to foreign Intelligence forces.

Apple accepted that the fact of the two-mile proximity was, of course, in itself a give-away. That, however, might not be realised for several days, by which time the innings could be finished.

The going was easy, Apple's stride was long, and there were no detours that needed to be made. He knew the way. When staying at Damian House he and others had often prowled the surrounding country.

He saw cows but no people. He passed through a spinney that was a riot of birdsong. On a gentle down-grade he sped forward into a run, feeling free and curiously light, sorry only that his speed was making the outing shorter.

The house came into view. It was Georgian and massive, a main body with two wings. There were lawns, a swimming pool, cricket pitch and tennis courts. Nominally the property was a holiday centre for the families of Armed Forces personnel. Its true use was by the Intelligence services, for hospitalisation, convalescence and some of the less arduous training courses.

Approaching from the rear, Apple came to an innocuous-looking hedge, broken and forlorn. It wouldn't have deterred a toddler for long. Apple, aware of the concealed warning-signal wires, cleared the hedge with a high, ranging jump. And that was the only line of protection. Fences, guards or dogs would have been a proclamation.

Unseen, though making no special effort to hide his presence, Apple skirted outbuildings. On a terrace beside the east wing, half a dozen people were lounging on deck-chairs. Laughter came from the direction of the pool. A couple strolled hand in hand. All the tennis courts were being used.

Apple headed that way, aiming for the front of the house. He wondered how his arrival would be viewed.

You didn't drop in casually at Damian House, unless you came from Upstairs.

Toward him on the path swung a man on crutches. One leg was missing. He was in his forties and had a thin, hard face. Apple recognised him at once. They had met several times, the first being here when Apple and other tyros on a Morse code course had been in awe of the older man, who was so high on the agent scale that he had treated the despot instructors like servants, yet was friendly toward their operative material.

They came close to one another on the path. Their eyes met. Apple knew he had been recognised, but the man on crutches gave no sign, swinging on past with the kind of polite nod you would give to a stranger.

The agent, Apple realised, had reached the point where every natural impulse had been smothered. He was not programmed to meet Appleton Porter. In the agent, deceit was the ruler. Smiles were acted. Left hand and right were permanently estranged. The game was inside you, always. You were complete. You were a star. You were alone.

Apple looked back, feeling sad and chilled. It was no help to him to know that the last time they had met, the agent had walked on two legs.

Apple went on. He reached the tennis courts and moved along beside them. His mind still partly on the complete agent, he was slow in responding when memory told him he was hearing a familiar voice. He stopped and looked at the players.

A second scan was needed before identification was clear. The man had changed his persona with the switch to tennis whites. Furthermore he was agile and eager, making up with dash for what he lacked in playing skill.

Moving close to that court, Apple stood and watched. It was some time before the man, coming to the net for a ball, looked over and saw him. He was not complete. His face twitched and he turned away too brusquely.

Apple went to a stack of folding chairs under a tree, opened out two, sat on one and lit a cigarette.

He thought about it.

The game was soon over. The man had lost his dash, though he still called out comments to his partner, who was a woman with a plaster cast on her left wrist.

The man signalled enough. They met at the net, came to the gate. The woman left. Twirling his racket airily, the man ambled to the tree. He said:

"Anyone, to coin a brand-new phrase, for tennis?"

"For Christ's sake," Apple said. "Do we have to go through all that crap?"

He might have known. He should have seen it from the start. The whole thing was straight out of espionage fiction. Trafalgar Square, the contact bits of crossword puzzle and ticket in hatband, the exchange of elaborate signals. The agent playing it blasé was probably his own idea, to soften the corn. But the rest of it was transparent —now. No genuine taxi would have stopped for a man who appeared to be drunk. Strongest: if the agent had been told where to go and what to do, he could also have been told the whole mission, there would have been no need for a second courier, for faceless Appleton Porter.

The man sat down. "Got a cigarette?"

They lit up. Apple asked, "How's the bug-bite or whatever?"

"Very funny."

"Someone made a mistake."

"Not me," the agent said quickly. "I'm clean. Lay it at Watkin's door. He ought to have super-thought of the possibility of you coming here, and sent me somewhere else."

Apple looked all around. "Will he find out I've been?"

"Depends. Depends on who sees you. Most here wouldn't tell their own mothers where they were born. But the staff, they're a bunch of finks. They think they're spies."

"Will it make any difference if Watkin finds out?"

"To you, you mean?"

"Yes."

"Maybe. He might pull you out."

"He couldn't," Apple said. "I've got rapport going there as strong as iron bars."

The agent shook his head. "That's not the point. You may start playing it all wrong now."

Apple didn't understand. He knew the what, but not the why. He hated to ask—one reason being that he might not be told—and he doubted if he could beat this more experienced man at bluffing, at pretending he already knew.

He felt sure it couldn't simply be language. At the flick of an index card, Upstairs could turn up a hundred operatives who were fluent in Russian. The same with someone unknown to the opposition. So if it wasn't a skill, could it be an *unskill*?

"I give in," Apple said. "I was chosen especially for this caper, and I can't see why. Not yet. It could take me another hour to figure it out, or I could call Watkin and say you'd dropped a few hints, or I could forget him and let you tell me."

The agent looked at him almost with admiration. "Russet, old boy, you will go far. You have the right degree of crappiness."

"Thank you."

"I'm surprised you haven't figured it out for yourself. It's no great cloak."

"So tell me."

"Will do. But be it on your own head. If you start playing it wrong, and you're almost sure to, you'll be pulled out so fast you'll get dizzy."

Apple took a long drag on his cigarette, dropped it, heeled it out. "Tell me."

"The routine," the agent said, "is called Fools-rush."

"Like bum's rush?"

"No, as in angels fearing to tread."

Apple nodded. He had been close. It was an unskill. He said, "Go on. I think I have the picture."

"You were sent in because you're a rank, screaming amateur. You'd be sure to do everything wrong from a pro point of view, but right as you, the semi-layman, saw it. Because of the clodhopper approach, you might just score where the smoothies had failed and are still failing. You'd muddle through, like the British, who're said to lose every battle but the last. You see?"

"Yes, I do. And the more I lurched about, the stronger my cover grew."

The agent raised a warning hand. "You're already talking in the past tense."

"I'll watch that," Apple said. "But is it so important, Fools-rush?"

"It is. It can't be acted, not for long. The pro's sure to slip up by making a clever move."

"I'm not convinced."

"Listen," the agent said. He put his cigarette out as if it

were in the way. "A while back in a certain city, the Mayflowers wanted to bug a certain embassy. The conference room. A big meeting was coming up. They tried all the brilliant tricks and even thought up some new ones. Nothing. Zero. So they had a try with Fools-rush."

"It worked?"

"Like a dream. They gave the job to a faceless one. Told him it wasn't important. He did what was first tried in 1910. He walked up to the front door, knocked and said he was from the electricity company, he'd come to check the wiring. They let him in. They had to. No agent would be that stupid."

"I get the message," Apple said. "Did he plant the bug?"

"Of course he did. In the chandelier." He laughed. "They didn't find it till the day before the conference."

"Well, there you are."

"But it was found by another amateur. A zealous searcher. The pros would've felt stupid looking in a bloody chandelier."

Apple asked, "Would it have made any difference in the long run, bug or no bug?"

The agent looked at him again. "Certainly not. Except to keep the game going. Ding-dong. From me, to you."

"It's the unexpected that counts nowadays, right?" Apple said. "There's so much of the double-think, so much of the he-knows-I-know-he-knows, that we're back to simplistics. At least for the time being."

"It'll work up again to the labyrinthine stuff."

Apple was silent for a minute. He said, "But sending a fool like me in must have its element of danger."

"Sure. If you flop, you flop hard."

"Which, coupled with all the fancy camouflage that's

gone into keeping me ignorant, can only mean that this thing is a lot bigger than it looks."

The agent said, "You're getting smart, Russet."

"In fact, it probably has nothing whatever to do with a defection."

"I don't know, but I'd say you were right. You have to be. Name defectors we want. The small-fry, forget it. They wipe off the Russian face for a maximum of three days. The papers have a ball. You know the kind of thing."

"Yes. Stewardess swims to freedom from visiting Soviet ship. Trumpets all round."

"Like as not, there won't be a word in the press when we get rid of the swimmer, who can only be a nuisance."

"Get rid of her?" Apple asked. He had that chill again.

"Remove the glamour and make life dreary. Either she asks to go back, or we convince her she should. It works about half the time."

"What happens to her when she gets home?"

"That's her business. She had no right to leave her motherland in the first place."

"It's a nice game."

The agent smiled. "I'm glad to hear you talk like that. You may pull it off yet."

Apple thought of the girl defector, her reception at home, her treatment by Hammers if they thought she had been sent back as an operative. He steeled himself.

"Okay," he said. "This is not a defection case. Do you know what it is?"

"No, I honestly don't. I know nothing about it. I had a job to do and I did it. That's all."

"You had me convinced with your performance."

"Thanks," the agent said, turning his head as a bell rang inside the house. "Time for tea."

Apple wondered if they still served that awful seed-cake that smelled of soap powder. He said, "I'd like you to do me a small favour, if that's all right. I want a check on a man calling himself Harry Wall." He described the South African. "He's hanging around the Oceansea Hotel, in case anyone wants to take a look at him."

"Call in. They'll check him for you."

"Watkin told me to keep mum except for a panic. I'm going to obey that to the letter, like any good greenhorn would."

"I'll see what I can do. I'll give you a call."

"Appreciate it," Apple said.

"Consider it business. One favour on the slate."

"That's fine with me."

The agent got up. "I don't imagine you'd care to show yourself, come in and partake of tea."

"You imagine correctly. But on the other hand, maybe that's just what a fool would do."

The agent said, "Don't lean too far in the opposite direction. And don't think big. Think corny. But best not to think at all. Act of instinct, if you can, now that you know."

"But I don't know. Not, that is, what I'm really looking for out there."

"If you did, you'd start doing all the right things that could be the wrong things. So far, obviously, you're okay."

"Why obviously?"

"Watkin hasn't pulled you out, has he?" the agent said, moving off. "So long, Russet."

On the drive back to London, the sole conclusion reached by Apple was that he had made a wise choice during his last term at university. He would not have been happy as a double agent.

All the ifs and buts, pros and cons, inverted thinking and backward viewing—they made his head ache. He wasn't sure if he were a greenhorn trying to think like a pro, or the semi-pro he basically was trying to think the way a pure pro would if he were trying to behave like a greenhorn.

It was too much. He wished he had never heard about Fools-rush. He didn't mind the insult. What bothered him was keeping his brain in straight.

The other factor he was glad to have clarified. Although his ignorance was a drawback, it was exciting to know that he had been dropped in at the deep end. It was also a little frightening.

Apple asked himself, carefully and seriously, if he would like to back out of the operation. He allowed a long time for an answer, needing the truth, not a flip comeback.

No, he didn't want out. He was happy to be in. Since that first call from Watkin he had felt, and still felt, more alive and real and special, and in closer touch with himself—the yearner inside. Danger heightened these emotions. He could see now why people stayed in the service, to and beyond the point of saturation, through injury and loss of limb. Superficially it was the schoolboy in adults; deeply, the primitive hunter in man.

They were right to call it a game, Apple thought. It was a bigger, grander, snobbier version of the one played by criminals, who could never go straight entirely, for that would be like hobbling an athlete and forcing him to

spend his prime years as a spectator. It was a game everyone wanted to play, and did so vicariously via the ever
popular fictional world of crooks and spies and private
eyes. It was a game whose secrecy made you feel clever,
superior. It was a game that supplied an outlet for
neuroses, while giving them absolution. Last and best of
all, it was a game that never ended.

He didn't want out.

In a suburb Apple stopped for a snack of tea and toast.
He didn't complain when they had no lemon marmalade.
Leaving the cafe he noticed a man selling the evening
newspapers, which reminded him of Jim Donald.
Strangely, that seemed a long time ago now.

Apple bought a copy of the *Comet*. The story was on
page three. It was disappointingly small, but the fact of
the ploy having come off was a plus.

Romeo and Juliev, smiled the heading. The rest told of
Mr. Appleton Porter's hopeless infatuation for a Russian
beauty who was virtually a prisoner, his neglect of work
so that he could stand under her window hoping for a
glimpse of his loved one, his near tearful telling of the
problem in an exclusive interview with the *Comet*'s own
Jim Donald.

Snowdrift. Dead.

After making a present of the paper to the news ven-
dor, Apple went back to the car and drove off.

He refused to think about it.

His watch told twenty past five when he parked near
the hotel. There were still people across the street from
there, including one pro-Soviet girl, her flag drooping,
some newsmen and the patient Harry Wall.

Apple walked briskly away from the car. He had almost
reached the hotel entrance when, as if by magic, a police

constable appeared in his path, bringing him to a sharp halt.

The constable was young, stern and scarred by acne. The silver point on top of his helmet was level with Apple's chin. He raised up on his toes to say, "One moment, sir, if you please."

"Yes, Officer?"

"You are Mr. Porter, I think."

Apple was nonplussed, though with a slant toward amusement. This had a suggestion of farce. "I am," he said. "But I don't understand how you know my name."

That seemed to make the policeman happy, or at any rate less stern. "I spotted you straight off, from the description."

"Good for you, Officer."

"Yes."

"And what can I do for you?"

"Well, sir. Official regrets and all that. It's not *our* doing, I'd like you to know."

"No," Apple said, amusement faded. "I suppose it's a flea in your ear from the Russian Embassy."

The policeman shook his head. "Hotel management. They're not going to make an issue of it. They're not going to do anything about what they referred to as a recent matter of unlawful entry. They just want you to stay away."

Apple asked a clear, "Why?"

"International incident. That's what they call it. See, they don't want one."

"Reputation of the hotel at stake?"

"There you have it, sir," the constable said.

Full marks to Kutuzov, Apple thought, beginning to feel cheerful. The reaction had the right smell to it.

Therefore his own, in return, should be soundly in the character of an innocent.

He said, "But this is outrageous."

"I got my job to do."

Apple argued. Voice raised, he threatened to see his Member of Parliament, consult his solicitor, go to the top in the Metropolitan Police. He put on a fairly good show. As expected, it failed to impress or sway the constable, who kept on shaking his head.

"You haven't heard the last of this," Apple said. Swinging around, he stalked off with a bounce that threatened to go too far. He eased it.

From behind came the clap of running footfalls. Apple wanted to look back. So do it, he told himself. Instinct.

He was beaten to the act by the runner coming alongside. It was Harry Wall, his blue eyes gleaming. Slowing to match Apple's walk he said:

"That was telling him. Good for you. I heard every word."

"It's an outrage."

"And I read that bit in the evening rag. Awful prose. But it has to be all to the good for us, especially if it goes out on wire to South Africa."

Apple seethed, "They can't get away with it."

"They can, actually," Harry Wall said. "It's legal. Every establishment reserves the right of admission. A loophole to keep out undesirables. The cops are on tap for it."

"You seem to know a lot about these things."

"I once studied law," he threw away. "But listen. This piece we're going to do between us. We can make it your personal account as told to me. It looks great."

They stopped beside the white Opel. Apple opened the

door and began on the project of folding his body down and in. "Sorry," he grunted. "Can't discuss it now. Too angry." He assured himself that his cover persona would respond this way, would think the journalist a nuisance. He would certainly believe he was a journalist. Fools don't have suspicious minds.

"Let's go for a drink somewhere till you calm down," the South African said. "I'll buy."

Apple shook his head, closed the door, started the motor, shot away with a leap that snapped his body back. As he drove by the constable he gave an outraged blast on the horn.

From the car-rental office Apple took a taxi home. He felt the need for fast movement, for quick scene-changes. His nerves were running briskly. He hoped he was being followed, but made no effort to check.

As Apple went into the flat the telephone started ringing. He strode to his old-fashioned living room and lifted the receiver. He cocked his head in curiosity when the caller identified himself as Professor Warden.

"Porter," he said. "Someone has just shown me an item in what purports to be a newspaper."

"I can explain, sir. I was on the point of calling you about that myself."

"Come come, there's no need to—um—"

"Apologise?"

"No. You don't have to . . ."

"Worry?"

"No, Porter, no," Professor Warden said. "*Lie.* That's the word."

Apple said, "I wasn't going to, sir. The truth of the matter is, this bit in the paper is a plant. Publicity. It was put there by the manager of Batewell Hall to stimulate business."

Soothingly: "Of course, of course."

"Really, sir. They do this kind of thing all the time."

"My dear boy," the linguist said. "Stop it. If you are enamoured of the lady—splendid, fine, excellent. High time you settled down. Bachelorhood is a bore." He went on to laud at length the state of marriage.

"Take all the time you want," he finished. "Don't rush it. There's many a slip twixt the cup and the saucer. Good-bye for now, my boy."

Lowering the receiver, Apple grinned with satisfaction. This side-effect of the newspaper story was an unexpected bonus. The Institute end of the business was now cleanly tied off.

Which made Apple think there might be other help to be won from the press—in respect of an idea about gaining admission to Batewell Hall. That, very likely, would be as plugged as the hotel.

He leafed through recent newspapers. The coverage on the parapsychological conference was concerned 80 per cent with the Russians. Also-rans mentioned politely were readers of papers on allied subjects, a Japanese duo doing ESP with Zener cards, an Austrian who cured headaches with his hands, an American hypnotist.

Apple got no ideas.

He sat at his typewriter. To the expense account he added flowers, coffee, lunch, sherry, hire car, tea, tea and toast, taxi. The list was growing nicely.

Apple sat on there. Somehow, he expected something to happen. Nothing did. He got up and went along to the bathroom.

Stripping, he took a fast shower, more for the action

than the wash. Before going back to the living room he tied a towel around his waist. Apple was a modest man.

He lit a cigarette and paced. His thoughts he gave to the operation, trying to figure out its true nature. He got nowhere. He wished he had discussed possibilities with the agent at Damian House.

Other people during the day came into his mind. He recalled reporter Jim Donald saying, "Why don't you give the girl a buzz on the blower?"—the approach of an innocent, like the man who had marched up to the embassy door.

Apple stopped pacing while he thought about it.

The cigarette burned his fingers. He tossed it in the fireplace and hurried back to the bathroom. His eyebrows were raised in smugness.

Five minutes later, dressed, he was listening to the call-signal ringing at the hotel switchboard. He sprawled in an easy chair. His left hand held a piece of cellophane, balled, which he had taken from around a box of corn flakes.

The call-signal ended, the receptionist said, "Oceansea Hotel. Good evening."

Apple said in a sparkless, efficient voice, "This is International. We're trying to put a call through to one of your guests. One moment, please." He flicked the receiver with a fingernail and then began to squeeze-release the cellophane to make a crackling sound. "Hello, Moscow. Are you still holding?" He twisted his mouth to one side and mumbled. Back in the first voice, cellophane silent, he said:

"Hello, Oceansea Hotel. This is a person-to-person from a Lazar Krupskaya. I'll spell that for you." He did

so. "He wishes to speak with someone of the same surname, first name Natasha. Clear?"

"Clear," the receptionist said. She sounded impressed.
"Hold the line. I'm dialling the room."

"Thank you," Apple said. Even if there had been a stop
on calls to Natasha as well as Olga, which he doubted,
this gambit would have lulled the receptionist into forget-
fulness. It would be an easy next step to have the big girl
pass the receiver over to her room-mate.

The receptionist said, "I have the party for you, International. Go ahead."

Apple said, speaking basic Russian, "Miss Natasha
Krupskaya? We have a call for you from Moscow."

"From Moscow?" the big girl asked. "Who's it from?"
She sounded incredulous. "Are you sure it's for me?"

"Yes, and the caller is Lazar Krupskaya. I'm putting
him on the line now." Apple crackled the cellophane
fiercely and said in a hollow tone, "Hello? Is that my little
one?"

"Uncle Lazar!" Natasha shrieked. "I don't believe it.
How thrilling. How fantastic. I'm beside myself. What are
you doing in Moscow? Never mind, don't waste time on
that. How are you? How's everybody?"

Apple said everyone was fine and asked how his favourite niece was getting along in the West. He wondered when it would be safe to judge that the receptionist
had stopped listening, bored with the foreign language.
He decided to give it two minutes at least. For making
the wrong guess between Moscow and Leningrad, he forgave himself.

Natasha was chattering on. How lucky that she happened to be in the room. She had just come in to get a
sweater—she and Olga were up on the roof. And Olga had

an admirer. Poor Kerinski had toothache again. They saw some gorgeous castles today and Comrade Kutuzov wouldn't let . . .

"Oh, but I'm forgetting. These names mean nothing to you, little uncle. Are you still there?"

Dreary at his wasted gambit—Olga being out—Apple said against a background of crackle, "I'm here, sweetness. Tell me about those people. Are they horribly respectable?" He thought he might as well try to salvage something from the call.

"Have you no news from home?"

"You, Natasha, are the family news at the moment."

She began chattering excitedly again. She described her colleagues, told of their personalities and foibles, filled in their backgrounds. Or, more exactly, she gave bits while jumping from one person to another.

Apple grew bored. Also his hand was getting tired from pumping the ball of cellophane. But he became alert when Natasha said:

"I'm different, of course. There's a gulf between us there. Anyway, Mother must have told you all this."

"Nothing. I know nothing. Or not much. You are the odd one out in the team, right?"

Natasha laughed. "No, Uncle Lazar, you have it the wrong way around. I'm among the five non-psychics. Only one person on the team is really a mind-reader. The rest of us, we're as mystified as the audience."

THREE

Apple sat staring into space. The telephone receiver in his hand was dead. Natasha had rung off after saying that he should forget what he had heard, it was a secret, she would get into trouble if anyone found out what she had said; though the reason she gave for ending the call was:

"This must be costing you a fortune, Uncle Lazar. Good-bye, good-bye. Love to everyone."

Only one member of the team was a mind-reader, Apple thought. He had thought it several times and now had it firm, ingested. The six people on the stage huddled in conference not to see if they could put together a coherent picture or message from the pieces they had separately received, but to be told what it was by the single ESP reader.

Question One: Who was it?

He had no idea. Except that it wasn't Natasha, and it wasn't the leader with the white moustache, probably, for that would be too obvious.

Question Two: Why?

That was even harder. There seemed to be no reason for carrying five dead-weights. To make less of the phenomenon by pretending it was the work of a group, not one extraordinary mind, was strangely un-Soviet. Furthermore, why create the need to guard six people instead of one?—unless the five themselves were guards.

That, Apple mused, was a possible answer. But a watchdog ratio like that was farfetched. It was also unnecessary. So the five could be there for stage-dressing, camouflage. That assumed to be true, the reason was obvious. Protection of another kind. Keeping the wolf out rather than keeping the sheep in. The Russians didn't want to risk losing their genius mind-reader, who was as useful to them in the propaganda competition as was a prize scientist in the space race.

Loss would be through a snatch by the West ("Did Eichmann swim to Israel from South America?"). Nobody was going to try to kidnap six people, and even if they did, and it came off, you'd need only one of the six to prove unco-operative afterwards for the whole thing to flop. If, however, it were known that the psychic power belonged to a single person, many countries would start to think in terms of the grab.

Apple got up, cradled the receiver, lit a cigarette and started to pace. He considered face as a reason why a country would want the medium. They would have to pass the snatch off as a defection, of course. That could be done, but then, if the medium continued publicly with his work, all propaganda credit would still belong to the Russians: the man was a Russian himself. Face wasn't it.

Apple squashed out his cigarette and went to the kitchen. Humming busily, he put two slices of bread in the toaster. He watched the appliance so that he could tell when it was about to make its noisy ejection, otherwise he would be startled.

It occurred to him in respect of Question One that he could use the Moscow call routine. Telephone each member of the team. By the recipient clearing himself—process of elimination—or by making an outright statement, or by a slip of the tongue, the identity of the psychic might be established. Apple resolved to find out the names of the other four members.

The toast clattered up. Apple coated the pieces thinly with butter, thickly with lemon marmalade. He perched his rump on the sink and began on the snack, crunching happily.

The medium, he thought, must have a use outside what amounted to show business; a job; the one he did when he wasn't performing, and the one his bosses wouldn't want him doing for anyone else. It would be a covert job. He had to be something in the nature of a secret weapon. What kind?

Apple had found no answer by the time he had finished the toast. He had, in fact, started cogitating like a pro, insidiously, clawing behind the new information, thinking along the lines of Natasha, having seen through the telephone trick, feeding him a tale, she being a Sickle in reality, and . . .

With relief he left the possible computations of that for a simpler, cleaner question. How was he going to get in Batewell Hall? Avoiding the pro approach, he went to the other extreme, back to full innocence. He wondered how a child would sneak into a picture house. How had he himself, for those Saturday afternoon cowboy movies? Well, he hadn't. He'd never had the nerve.

But, Apple remembered, he had known boys who used to get in regularly for free. And the way they had done it was not during the mass entrance, but long before the movie started.

Apple snapped a look at his watch, pushed off from the sink and left the kitchen. Thirty seconds later he was leaving the flat. He closed the door behind him, paused, reflected.

Nodding, he went back inside. By the telephone he got the directory and turned to the yellow pages. When he had numbers jotted down, he began making calls. He made five in all. Each followed the same pattern, once he had got past the switchboard:

"Hello. Is that Jim Donald?"

"No. Wrong man, wrong paper."

Pretending to misunderstand: "It doesn't matter. You can tell him when he comes in. It's about that exclusive story today. You know, Romeo and Juliev. The English-man and one of the Russian mind-readers. Well, tell him there could be an interesting development tonight at Batewell Hall and he shouldn't miss being there. Okay?"

Out of the flat again Apple trotted downstairs. He stopped by the hall table. There was a letter for him among the line-up of mail, which was newly delivered. Apple toyed with the idea of misplacing his letter to see what happened, but decided against the to-catch-a-thief routine. It was too smart.

The letter, a bill, he put in his pocket as he went out to the street.

Thief, he mused. There was something about that word that tickled a chord. Not memory—a hint. Thieves fall out? Thick as thieves? Time's a thief? Or was it something to do with criminals in general?

Apple thought about it.

The answer came when he was swinging up his arm to signal to a taxi. A lie-detector. That's what the Russian psychic could be used for, and most likely was when he wasn't helping to give the West a dig in the eye with the parapsychological act. He could sit in on interrogations,

on talks, on casual-seeming conversations. There would
be no cables attached to the arms. It wouldn't be known
about. He would sit there quietly and read the subject's
mind. He was a human polygraph.

The glass doors at the front of Batewell Hall were
locked. Inside, a man was pushing a brush across the floor
of the lobby, plodding inscrutably back and forth. He
looked to have been doing it all his life.

Apple discarded the idea of a try at getting the man to
let him in, either by bribe or bluff. For one thing, he knew
it was hard to con a fool. For another, there was the
official adage: *The closer to the bottom of the job scale,
the higher the level of incorruptibility.*

Apple moved on. He went down the alley to the stage-
door. It gave not a fraction of an inch when he turned the
handle and pressed. Farther along he came to a row of
emergency exits, double-doors which he knew opened
outward, operated by crush-bars. No hope there, except
for the expert.

Next came a stretch of wall that rose smooth and high.
It ended at a corner, around which Apple found a drainpipe. Square and solid, it went up twenty feet to a ledge.

Apple began to climb.

He used feet, knees, elbows and ·hands, gripping only
on the sides of the pipe because it lay flat to the wall.
Half-way up, he wished he was down. But returning
would take almost as much effort as going on. He went
on.

The ledge came within reach. Sweating, Apple grasped
it and chinned himself up. He got over onto a flat roof.
The main body of the building still soared above him.

Nearby were three windows. The middle one was open.

Apple climbed through into a room sided with suitcases in stacks. He tiptoed to the door. It was firmly locked.

Back out on the flat roof, Apple saw another drainpipe. It was round, and went up ten feet to a trough along jutting eaves. That nasty outcropping gave Apple the qualms, which he ignored by whistling.

The climb was easy, with Apple being able to grip around the pipe, but when he came to the eaves he realised that this bit was beyond his skill. He went down again.

Plaintively he gazed through the open window at the locked door. He scowled at the suitcases; then blessed them with a sudden smile and scrambled into the room.

He started tossing cases through the window. All empty, they bounced quietly on the flat roof. One went too far and sailed down to the alley. Apple didn't care.

When the room was cleared he went out and set about building a stairway beside the drainpipe. He enjoyed the task. It was like playing with blocks. He had no need to tell himself to take his time, make a careful job of it.

He started up on all fours. The stack swayed. He jiggled it back into the true, and went on jiggling in the way he had seen ladder-climbers do in a circus. His stairway held upright. At the top he edged carefully onto the roof-tiles.

Standing in a forward crouch, he went up the incline. Its apex was at right-angles to the bottom of another roof. This one had dormer windows. It also had a gradient so steep that Apple didn't get the qualms, for he had no intentions of going up there.

He was hoping that the suitcase stairway would hold for the return journey, while, at the same time, he found himself crawling up onto the roof.

He didn't believe it. Yet he kept on going, now flat out in an X. He shuffled upward and sideways, aiming for the first of the windows.

Apple was stiff with fear. His sweat turned to a cold slime. The insanity of his action was worsened by him knowing it wasn't for Queen and country, but pride. So badly did he want to look down that he groaned in the effort of resisting.

He forged on, moving slowly. A light wind was blowing up here and it slapped at his clothes, as well as sending dust into his eyes. He blinked constantly.

Although he made no slips, Apple wasn't assured. The fear stayed on his shoulder like a faithful parrot; it seemed to be whispering doubts in his ear.

He rested, shuffled, rested, shuffled. It took him ten minutes to cover three yards. When his hand touched the ledge of the window, he felt as if he had run the mile, backwards. But recovery was fast. He pulled himself closer and took measure of the situation.

The window was of small panes and in two halves. The central catch was a handle. If that was the only locking device there would be no problems, but that itself was problem enough.

Apple carefully twisted himself sideways. He bent his leg up, stretched an arm down. Hand touched shoe. Fumbling, he got the lace untied, drew the shoe off and straightened.

He inched higher in front of the window—and became a better target for the wind. It flapped his tie in his face. Using two fingers of the shoe-holding hand, he managed to get the cavorting tie in his mouth.

Apple tapped the heel of the shoe against a centre pane. The glass cracked at once. On the second blow, weakly made out of fear of the big movement, the glass broke away from its frame and tinkled inside. Apple stuffed his shoe in after it.

Next, his hand went through, grasped the handle, turned it down. He pushed. The window stayed solid. Apple closed his gritty eyes.

Before fear could start to rant, however, he thought to try the handle upward. That did it. The window eased open prettily.

Dropping inside a storage attic, Apple gave a feeble laugh of relief, told himself he hadn't really been in the least bit scared, tried to stand and felt his legs dither. He sat for the duration of a cigarette.

Putting his shoe on, he went to the door. It was unlocked. It led Apple to a passage and to steps going down. The level below served as access to the gallery of the auditorium. There were washrooms. In the men's, Apple spent some minutes sponging with wet paper towels at his clothes to get the dirt off, or disguised under dampness. He washed his hands and face, cupped water to his eyes.

Feeling perky and proud, he went back upstairs. In the attic, sitting behind a pile of boxes, he lit another cigarette and gave his mind once again to the matter of a human lie-detector.

The medium would not, he realised, be able to read everything that passed through the subject's mind, and perhaps not any particular thing. Thought moved too swiftly for that, except when controlled for the purpose of reading. For instance, people didn't normally muse, I am going to climb that wall. It was an association of ideas and impulses. But what the medium would be able to receive was gist, and change of thought-direction from the straight to the crooked, or the reverse. Deception would be seen, and all without the subject's slightest suspicion that he was being listened in to. It was a secret weapon of the highest order. A human polygraph was worth his weight in spies' brains.

There was another round of applause. When it had died down, and its aftermath of coughing had faded, a lone female voice began to speak. Although it came faintly to Apple, he recognised that it belonged to the spokeswoman of the Russian group.

Apple was on the ground floor, in a passage at the side of the auditorium. Without seeing anyone he had made his way down after the programme had started.

On tiptoe he moved to the nearest swing doors. He eased one half open until he had made a one-inch crack. Through it he saw the stage. It was as last night: spokeswoman, and the six team members sitting together.

Also in the same place was Kutuzov, at the far end of the front row. He sat semi-sideways, taking in both stage and seating. His posture gave him a Tzar-like arrogance.

As well as he could in the gloom and with his view restricted, Apple searched faces in the audience. He could pick out no Hammers or Sickles.

"The Union of Soviet Socialist Republics," the spokeswoman said, "is happy that its experiments in this field can serve only to create a better understanding among the world's peoples." She was repeating her neat speech.

Apple wondered if it was deliberate, the choice of this woman who showed not a hint of personality. Plump, dowdy and unfashionably dressed, she stood there stolidly in her high-heel boots, mouthing words like a robot. It all helped to play down the phenomenon as nothing out of the Russian ordinary.

By comparison, the team looked ready to shake the nearest hand. They were relaxed, sitting in a half-circle, with the two girls in the middle. Olga's prettiness and petiteness were increased by her proximity to Natasha.

The spokeswoman was plodding toward the end of her speech. Apple sank to his haunches. He quietly pushed the door farther open, crept through and stopped beside the wall. He stayed in the low crouch. Those people close at hand who had turned to watch his entrance soon gave their attention back to the stage.

The woman in the trouser suit adjusted her blue-tinted glasses. She said, "I would like to ask a member of the audience to act as a volunteer."

Apple had risen on the third word. By the tenth he was striding down the middle aisle. He was glad to see he had no competitors. He fixed his eyes on Kutuzov.

The man with the silver teeth stared. He began to get up. He was in an upright stoop by the time Apple reached him, and, with a nod, strode on past. He went up the steps.

The team smiled; the girls warmly. The spokeswoman appeared offended, her mouth drawn tight. She looked toward the front row, as if in search of guidance.

Apple went to her and took hold of her hand. He gave it an efficient shake. Loudly he said, "My name's Appleton Porter. I'm a philologist." He walked to the chair, where he sat down firmly.

The audience was mumbling. Apple smiled at the team. Olga gave a brief wave, fingers wriggling. The big girl giggled.

The spokeswoman came over. For a moment Apple

thought that she was going to ask him to leave. But she turned to the audience and explained what she wanted the subject to do. Next she stood beside the chair. The touch of her hand on his shoulder was not gentle.

Apple looked at the six people. They were leaning forward, sober now. Not one stood out as being in a particularly profound state of concentration.

Slowly, word for word, in Russian, Apple thought, *Olga Goliski is the prettiest girl I know.*

The team looked at him for ten more seconds. They exchanged glances, still serious, leaned back and put their heads together. Abruptly, they laughed.

The man with the white moustache got up and said in his own language, "His thought was that our girls are very pretty."

The spokeswoman translated, Apple nodded, the audience broke into clapping and laughter. Apple wondered if the pluralisation of the message had been due to error in reception, or deliberate; and, if the latter, was the reader merely being a considerate diplomat, or something more devious?

The spokeswoman pushed on Apple's shoulder, at the same time pulling on the chair. He found himself standing as the woman asked loudly:

"Could we have another volunteer, please?"

Apple said to her, "Why can't I have more turns?"

"You were here last night. People might suspect collusion. Good-bye, Mr. Porter."

Apple went to the team. He solemnly shook hands with each member. To Olga he whispered, "Hello."

"Hello, Appleton," she said. "We thank you for the compliment."

He nodded. "See you in a minute." Turning, he walked

away. But he didn't go to the front of the stage. He went
into the wings.

There were twenty-five to thirty people backstage. Two
were talking to themselves, rehearsing speeches. Several
were sitting around a hamper and looking at drawings.
Another group included two Japanese. There were uniformed staff. A Hammer and the stocky Sickle stood near
the stage-door entrance. Three obvious reporters lounged
together, being watched by a fourth, who was Jim
Donald.

Apple stopped. For a moment he went unnoticed.
Then, at the same time, he was seen by the Sickle, Jim
Donald and a man in a tuxedo. They all came across, arrived in a bunch, and all started talking at once. Because
of the nearness of the stage, they had to whisper.

The man in the tuxedo, apparently the manager, asked
Apple what he was doing here. Jim Donald asked if he
had seen the item in the newspaper. The Sickle grated in
Russian, "What is the meaning of this, Mr. Porter?"

There followed confusion, which worsened to farce
when Kutuzov came backstage and strode over to join the
group. The flying whispers sounded like rapiers being
swiped through the air. Everyone else watched with interest. Some drew closer. The reporters looked hopeful.

The manager kept waving his arms for silence while
hissing questions. Kutuzov ordered the Sickle to tell the
manager in English that Apple must have got in without
a ticket. Jim Donald, pencil poised, asked about new de-
velopments in the romance. A staff member approached
and stared at Apple menacingly.

The reporters and others edged closer still. Apple was
busily switching back and forth from one language to an-

other, purposely using the wrong one for the wrong person. It seemed to make no difference. He changed to Portuguese.

Voices rose under the cover of a round of applause from the auditorium. The clapping died away, the voices stayed high. The manager began shushing and pushing. He got the people moving and herded them away from the stage. On the way they collected the reporters and several others.

They all came to a halt by an iron stairway. Calm settled. The Sickle got her message over to the manager. He told Apple he would have to leave. Apple folded his arms and shook his head.

Kutuzov said, "I hope you realise that you are damaging East–West relations."

"All I'm trying to do is improve my relations with the young lady."

"You have no right even to try."

"Why not?" Apple asked. "I think you're being more than a little ridiculous."

Kutuzov showed his teeth. "Olga Goliski, my friend, is engaged to be married."

Jim Donald asked, "What's he saying, what's he saying?"

Kutuzov: "What does the jackal want?"

Apple and the Sickle began translating. Others talked. The staff member came and put a hand on Apple's arm. One of the reporters took a picture.

Silence fell at the flash. The man with the silver teeth was quietly livid. "This has to stop," he seethed. He turned to the Sickle: "Tell that man in the waiter's uniform that if he doesn't throw this hop-pole out, we will."

Before the woman could obey, there was another burst

of clapping, and in the wings appeared the mind-reading team. Led by the spokeswoman, they came over to the stairway. Confusion started again.

It was Apple who ended it. Shaking off the employee, he raised both arms above his head and brought his hands together in a loud clap. Quiet dwindled into place over the surrounding crowd of thirty-odd people, the involved and the observing.

"Ladies and gentlemen," Apple said, looking around with a smile. "All this fuss is a storm in a teacup." He spoke in English. The Sickle was translating in an undertone. "I am here merely to walk Miss Olga Goliski"—gesturing toward the girl—"back to her hotel, which is what she and I agreed on this morning."

Olga looked surprised, but reacted well, changing to a smile as Kutuzov pushed his way toward her. He asked, "Is that right?"

"Yes, Comrade. More or less. We agreed that it would be nice to have a walk. I said I would ask you."

"But you didn't."

"I forgot."

Apple translated loudly for Jim Donald. One of the reporters asked, "Does she have to have permission to go for a walk, for God's sake?"

Apple translated that as well. Across Kutuzov's plain face flitted a variety of emotions. Apple wouldn't have believed him capable of expressing so much. But he could understand the man's predicament. It was security versus a bad, antagonistic press; it was loss of power over the team, loss of face in front of his KGB subordinates; it was dread of castigation from Moscow, and that could mean his whole future.

Apple sympathised. He tried to think of a loophole he could offer to the man with the silver teeth.

With the Sickle again interpreting, Kutuzov said, his face back to normal, "There is no question of permission. All our people are free. Which also means being free of nuisance. The point to be considered is rest after the trials of concentration."

"Walking clears the head," Apple said. He was no longer sympathising.

Kutuzov brushed his wart. "Walking, my friend, is, as everyone knows, a dangerous thing in the cities of the West."

A reporter said, "Got to get their bloody politics into everything, haven't they?" No one translated.

The man with the silver teeth spread his arms, offering, "There are muggers, murderers, white-slavers, body-snatchers, rapists, cut-purses. These things are not allowed in the Soviet Union."

The reporter asked, "You mean, like, they're illegal?" No translation.

"Therefore, naturally, one is greatly concerned at the prospect of a young girl walking in the streets of this city which is notoriously rife with crime."

Apple: "She wouldn't be alone."

"Even so," Kutuzov said, "it is a matter of concern. You must have protection on your outing."

Apple's mind did a double-take. "You mean she can go?"

"Go? Go? But of course she can go. What a foolish question. Whatever made you think she couldn't?"

Twenty yards ahead crawled a car that held two Hammers. Ten yards ahead walked the Sickle. Keeping level on the opposite side of the street was Kutuzov. Behind came Jim Donald and one other reporter (their colleagues had yawned and left). Trailing was a second Hammer-driven car.

"It's a pity," Olga was saying, "that the rest of the team couldn't have come as well. They would have enjoyed this."

"Yes," Apple said absently. He was wondering if the KGB had a directional microphone going, to pick up the conversation. He decided not. There hadn't been enough time for such an arrangement.

Apple came alert to what the girl had just said. It was a cue. He asked, "What's the team leader's name, by the way? The man with the white moustache."

She told him, along with the names of the other males. He rapidly formed mnemonics by matching each name with a similar sounding one that belonged to a film star.

Olga darted out of line to go to the window of a dress shop. It was the second time she had done this. Apple waited impatiently. He felt like a husband.

"If we keep stopping," he said, "Kutuzov might make you go in a car."

They walked on. Olga praised his command of her language and asked about his knowledge of Russian literature. Apple slipped around that. There wasn't much time.

"Olga," he said, "do you ever think you might like to live outside the Soviet Union?"

She shrugged. "Sometimes. But I'd miss my work." She began to tell of her typist job.

Apple cut in, "What I mean is, you have no family ties."

"There's my sister."

Apple was irked by his mistake. He should have asked

about family, not stated. But the girl hadn't picked it up, it seemed. "You have a sister?"

"We're not close," Olga said dismissingly. "Do you know what Nikolai says?"

"About your sister?"

"No, about you. He says that when you came onstage last night he thought you were KGB testing us."

"Testing you for what?" Apple asked, playing the innocent, but making careful note of this. Was Nikolai the mind-reader? Was he the one who had picked up, and blocked, the message about freedom?

Forgetting that he had just asked a question, Apple bluffed with another, "Is he the one that Natasha mentioned, married and with two children?"

"No, not Nikolai. He's married to his stamp collection. He would have brought it with him even, if that could have been managed. But it's too valuable to take around."

"Really?"

"Anyway, he hasn't been letting the grass grow under his feet. He's made contacts here."

Apple felt uncomfortable. "Contacts?" he asked in a hurt tone of voice.

"One in particular. A dealer called Household. Kutuzov has let them meet several times."

Apple knew in the marrow of his every bone that Household was competition. He said, "I don't understand why Kutuzov allows that but keeps trying to get rid of me."

Primly: "Philately is a very serious matter."

"Mmm."

Brightly: "But let's not talk of dreary things. Tell me about yourself, your comrades, your sweethearts."

"I have no girl friends. Not romantic ones." As Olga

began veering toward a shop, he took her arm and held onto it. "Listen. I hope *you* don't think I'm KGB."

"Oh no. Nikolai is paranoid. Why are you without a girl friend?"

"I've been too busy. But you don't seem to have had the problem, Olga."

She looked up at him with a quizzical smile. "Who told you about my boyfriends? Natasha, I expect. It is true that I like a lot of admirers." She went on to tell in detail of her most recent flirtations.

Apple asked at last, "Isn't there one that you're engaged to?"

Olga laughed. "Heavens over us, no. I have no fiancé." She again headed toward a shop window. Apple went with her, looking around when they stopped. The rest of the procession had also halted. The third reporter had deserted; Jim Donald was now across the street, trying to talk to Kutuzov.

"This Nikolai then," Apple said. "He's different from the rest of you."

"Yes. More serious. I like that one with the low neckline. What d'you think?"

"Very pretty. You know, you could have lots of dresses like that if you lived in the West."

Olga giggled. Apple asked, "What's funny?" She gave him a twinkling glance. "Kutuzov told us we had to come to him at once if anyone talked to us like that."

"And will you?"

"Course not, silly. They're all paranoid."

"As badly as Nikolai?"

"Worse," Olga said. "I love that dark green one at the back with the puff sleeves. What d'you think?"

Apple was about to press on with questions relating to

the hot prospect Nikolai, when he realised the cue, the repeated cue. He was amazed with himself for not having come up with this idea sooner. It was dear old process of elimination.

He asked, "The green dress?"

"Yes, at the back there."

"You want to have my opinion of it?"

"Yes, please," Olga said.

Apple formed a sentence in his mind and thought it slowly: *There is a spider on your hair.* Olga stayed as she was, gazing through the window. Apple worked carefully through the sentence again.

The girl looked up at him. "Well? Tell me. Do you like it?"

"No," he said.

They shook hands outside the hotel. Olga went inside gaily, followed with less spirit by the rest of the procession's Russian element, Kutuzov returning Apple's nod coldly.

Jim Donald came up. "Well?" he asked. "Any progress in the romance department?"

"Not much."

"You know, I think the story's gone dead. Now, if a fight had started back there at the theatre . . ."

"Sorry about that."

"You weren't thinking of trying to get in the hotel, were you?"

Apple looked at the constable sitting in the lobby. "I can't oblige you, Donald."

"There must be some angle I can use. Will you go to Batewell Hall again tomorrow night?"

"They won't be there. This was their last time. They

rest for a couple of days and then perform in Edinburgh."

"Jesus," the reporter said. "Edinburgh. There's been no news out of that place since Burke and Hare."

"Kutuzov is of the opinion that they're alive and well and still snatching bodies," Apple said. "See if you can make a story out of that."

"Oh sure."

"Good night."

Apple set off to walk home. He went at a smart pace. Whether or not he was being tailed was of no particular interest to him. His mind was full of Nikolai and the supposed stamp-dealer called Household. Apple had the feeling that he had joined in a race. He didn't much care for that. He walked faster.

At home he fixed himself a sherry on the rocks. Sprawled in a chair, he gazed at the ceiling between sips. Drink finished, he got up and went toward the kitchen to prepare a meal, doubling back agilely when the telephone rang.

He lifted the receiver. A man said, "You may recognise my voice."

"Yes. I asked you about the Great Wall of somewhere or another."

"Right, by Harry," the agent said. He chuckled. "Aren't we the cute ones though?"

"Maybe. If, that is, you found out something for me about Harry Wall."

"Not a thing, Russet, and I got an inter-service guy—who claims to know everyone in the world—to take a look at your man. He's a mystery, therefore maybe straight. But don't bet any money on it."

"Okay. Thanks for trying."

"No thanks, thanks," the agent said. "You owe me."

"As you like," Apple said. "Oh, by the way. There's a matter I'm curious about. You could probably tell me, if it's not contravening the Official Secrets Act."

"Ask and ye shall find out."

"A certain person with one leg. Not too far from you. I'd like to know what happened."

There was a silence before the agent said, "As a matter of fact, he was Back-up man on a Fools-rush."

Apple lowered the receiver slowly. He wished he hadn't asked, but appreciated his good sense in not going further and asking what had happened to the fool.

Then he noticed something that drove the information from his mind, as well as making the hair on the crown of his head tingle unpleasantly.

A drawer of the desk was not fully closed. It stuck out half an inch. Apple was fussy about such things. He wouldn't have left the drawer like that.

He stepped away. Carefully he looked around the room. The animal tingle of his hair continued. A chair was in a slightly different position. The fringe on a Persian rug lay over on the pile. The folds of the drapes were too neat.

Apple went into other rooms. They had the same signs. And this wasn't the day for the weekly charwoman. Nor did burglars try to hide evidence of their visits. The flat had been searched, for evidence.

Apple went to wash his hands and face. He felt dirty. Next, he made another tour. The tingling stopped and he began to see the value to himself of the furtive visit. There was nothing here to hurt his cover, and the fact that someone had gone to this trouble to check showed he was at the head of the pack.

Apple did wonder about his expense account, sticking

up from the typewriter. But that, surely, could be seen as legitimate: the tidy-minded bachelor itemising the cost of his courtship.

Whistling, Apple went into the kitchen. He prepared a plate of cold cuts, a stale sausage well coated with sauce, tomatoes, olives, and chocolate biscuits which he had allowed to go soft. After exchanging his suit-coat for the tartan robe, he rubbed his hands and sat down to eat.

He wondered if he too had a Back-up. Most likely, yes. If so, there were several possibles—if letting the presence be seen was permitted.

It was gradually, while eating, that Apple began to feel uncomfortable. It was like a heat rash beginning to take hold. He stared into space and chewed slower and slower. When knowledge caught up with instinct, the heat rapidly gathered strength and he was engulfed in a tremendous blush.

On coming out of the snowdrift, alive, Apple pushed his plate away and lit a cigarette. He had nearly made a fatal mistake. He had been going to ignore the fact that someone had been in his home. That's what an agent would do, but not an innocent.

The visit, Apple mused, had been a combination search and test. That was obvious now, for, had the opposition been working in normal fashion, the place would have been turned over so expertly that only another expert would have stood a chance of realising it. Not a speck of dust would have been out of place. There would have been none of these signs of a visitor, which had been left deliberately.

Apple squashed out the cigarette on his plate because he hated that kind of thing. Punishment over, he got up and went around the flat destroying subtleties. He pulled

drawers farther out, scattered linen, tossed papers on the
floor, twisted a mattress sideways on its bedstead.

Satisfied with his work, he went to the telephone and
called the police.

In a flustered tone he told the answering voice that he
had been robbed. "Burglars. In my flat. Come quickly.
Do you hear me? I've had thieves in."

He let the voice talk him to calmness, gave his name
and address, rang off with another plea for haste.

After putting on his jacket again, mussing his hair and
pushing the knot of his tie to one side, Apple left the flat
and went down to the street.

He began to pace out a stretch of pavement in front of
the door. There was a sprinkling of passers-by, but Apple
didn't look too hard. What robbery victim could spare a
thought for anyone other than himself?

Silently, moving at a steady speed, a patrol car appeared. It came along the street and drew into the kerb.
Even before the two uniformed men got out, Apple was
telling them about his burglary. He did so with agitated
gestures. He knew his performance was convincing because of the bored look the officers exchanged.

"All right, sir," one said. "Let's go up. You make us all
a nice hot cup of tea while we poke around. The CID
boys'll be along soon for prints and a statement."

"This way," Apple said. "Imagine this happening to
me."

"How much they take you for?"

"What? Oh, nothing. I never keep money in the house
and there's nothing else of value."

"It's your lucky day, sir."

"Lucky?" Apple echoed, putting a hand to his brow.

"My God, Officer, someone broke into my home and you call that lucky? I could've been murdered."

The men exchanged another look.

Apple awoke late the next morning. It had been eleven o'clock before the detectives had got through with their dusting for latent prints and their questions (they seemed to find the lack of theft curious and made him double check); midnight before he had finished cleaning up the black powder and getting the ink off his fingers from having his own prints taken.

Apple showered, put on his robe and fixed his usual breakfast. While eating he worked at remembering which film actors he had used as mnemonics to remind him of the names of the male Russians in the psychic act. Two came quickly, the third was awkward, for the fourth he had to go through the alphabet and follow each letter with vowel-sounds.

Armed with his ball of cellophane, Apple sat by the telephone. He dialled the hotel. After he had gone through his opening pitch as the International operator, the switchboard told him:

"Sorry, the Russian party's not available. They checked out early this morning."

"Oh," Apple said densely.

"Is that all, operator?"

"No. Listen, miss. This call from Moscow is most urgent. Could you tell me where the Russians went, please?"

"I couldn't, sorry. They left no forwarding address. Maybe Edinburgh. That's where they're appearing Monday."

Apple mumbled his thanks and put down the receiver.

He felt empty. Not flabbergasted or thwarted or enraged; just empty. He didn't know what to do next.

What he finally did was get out an Automobile Association book and start dialling Edinburgh hotels. He asked each what time the Russian party was due to check in. From the seventh desk clerk he learned:

"Mid-day on Monday, sir. We have four single rooms reserved."

"That can't be right," Apple said. "There's at least a dozen of them."

"Ah, in that case, it's the Black Gordon you want. We're a wee bit humbler at the Anvil. It seems to be a matter of the Orwells: everyone equal but some more equal than others."

"So who are your guests?"

"One's down as a baggageman, another as a wardrobe mistress. I don't know about the other two."

When Apple disconnected he dialled the Black Gordon Hotel. The receptionist told him that the Russian party would be arriving Monday at five o'clock in the afternoon, on the express from London.

Which, Apple thought as he went to dress, meant that the two days of rest were being spent somewhere in the city or the Home Counties. Or so it looked.

Apple left the flat and went downstairs. There was no mail. Outdoors, wearing a preoccupied expression, he walked along to Tottenham Court Road and turned north. He passed two telephone boxes, went in a snack bar and sat gloomily over a coffee for a quarter hour, drumming his fingers.

He retraced his steps. After going by the second public telephone, he stopped as if just taken by a bright idea, went back and entered the booth.

He called in. Several minutes of fencing went by before he was told, "Ring back in half an hour."

"This is an emergency. He better be in by then."

"Good-bye."

"For now," Apple said, disconnecting with a flourish.

He turned to find a woman in the half-open door. She was middle-aged and dressed poorly. She said, "You takes your time on the blower, mate."

"Was it interesting?"

"Don't be snotty. Now, move on and let someone else have a go. Me daughter's sick in orspital."

Apple came out and walked off. He told himself the woman was probably straight, and not to look back, because if she wasn't, then all to the good—only to someone on his own side would his talk have made sense.

The woman reminded him of there being two levels of hotel accommodation for the Soviets. He found that odd. It could so easily be used against them as a weapon of derision. The arrangement was a poor one.

It nagged at Apple's mind, joining another faint prod: that something had been said on the walk to the hotel last night that was important. Unfortunately, he lacked total recall. He only remembered gists.

Near the British Museum, Apple noticed the bookstore. He crossed to it and entered. As before, the place was empty except for the woman.

Apple browsed among the shelves and racks. At length he chose a paperback on the haunting of Borley Rectory. He took a fancy to the cover.

At the desk, while giving him his change, the woman said, "Someone was asking about you yesterday, sir."

"A friend?"

"No. He thought he knew you. He asked if you were

the Mr. Jones who worked at the bank. I said I didn't know who you were, I'd only ever seen you once."

Apple would have winced at the Jones except for remembering that simplistics were in at the moment. He asked:

"This man, what did he look like?"

The woman gave a description. It could have fitted anyone who wasn't out of the ordinary. But Apple mused that the query was another mark in his favour.

Book pocketed, he left the shop and headed in a southerly direction. The Saturday streets were busy. As earlier, he had no idea if he were being tailed. He intended assuming that he was, however.

In a shopping arcade he found the type of public telephone he preferred—one with a cowl. He called in. Angus Watkin came on the line with, "I hope you're not phoning from home."

"Of course not, sir," Apple said. He held back "Do you think I'm an idiot?" because it might not be taken as an attack but treated as a question, and answered.

"Tell me your emergency, Porter."

"Our Russian friends have left the Oceansea Hotel. I need help to find where they've gone."

"I see."

"I don't suppose you happen to know, do you, sir?"

"Naturally I know. The party is obliged to report its movements to the authorities."

Apple smiled. "That's a break." He stopped smiling when Watkin went on:

"But I have no intentions of telling you, Porter. The KGB know, of course, that I know, so if you show up there smartly you'll stand a chance of losing whatever you might have gained. Find them yourself, if you can, and if you want to, but let it be seen that it was all your own work."

Apple let a silence grow. Angus Watkin asked, "Have you anything to report?"

"A lot," Apple said tartly. "But I haven't the time now. Over and out." He disconnected.

Strolling along the arcade, his cursing of Watkin finished, Apple came to the conclusion that it would be safer for his cover if he didn't find the Russians, or at any rate until tomorrow at the earliest. But he had to show willingness.

Apple took a cab to the Oceansea Hotel. There were no loiterers across the street, no police at the entrance, no Hammers or Sickles inside.

The receptionist repeated what the switchboard had said: the Soviet group had gone without leaving a forwarding address. Apple offered to pay for information.

The clerk shook his head. "You could have it for nothing. I honestly don't know." He added obscurely, "Reds don't tip."

"One more thing," Apple said, holding himself back from leaving. "The lower orders of the party, they were staying somewhere else, right?"

"I believe so, yes. Four or five of them."

"Could you tell me where, by any chance?"

"I'm afraid not."

Just as well, Apple thought. It would be tempting, but probably damaging, to poke around there. He asked:

"Was the Russian party split into two groups because you didn't have enough space here?"

The clerk said, "No, the rooms here were reserved months in advance. We could have accommodated four hundred." He shook his head. "Four hundred non-tippers. Think of that."

Apple gave him a pound note in the silent name of Olga. He left the hotel looking slightly harried.

Apple spent the rest of the day prowling the city. He made enquiries about Russian tourists at two private bus companies and three hire-car firms. He asked in travel agencies if they knew which places in town or country were popular with visitors from the Communist countries. He had a meal in a restaurant called the Golden Samovar, where the Italian waiters were dressed like Cossacks.

Apple decided that tomorrow at noon he would pry the party's whereabouts out of Angus Watkin by telling him what he had learned about the single mind-reader. Meanwhile he would think up some blundering way to explain how he had found the group.

He sat on a bench in Hyde Park, supposedly to rest and read. When he got up to go, he left the book there, as if by accident. He knew that watchers would suspect a drop, and spend many weary hours waiting for the collector, though Apple hoped that the innocent who would eventually, inevitably appropriate the book wouldn't be given a hard time. Should the paperback by some fluke go unclaimed, the watchers would take it themselves, spend more hours on minute examinations, and find it innocuous. It was all grist to his cover, and a pain to the other side. It would seem strange if he did nothing at all that could be suspect.

Apple went to the main museums, asking what foreign groups had visited or were due to visit. The same enquiries he made at an exhibition hall, two theatres and the Tower of London. He didn't forget to pat his pockets and thereby show realisation of book loss.

He went to the police station nearest the Oceansea Hotel. With a thump of his fist on the counter, he demanded to be told where the Russian visitors had moved to. He was shown out.

He bought a copy of the *Comet*. It had no further installment of the Romeo and Juliev saga. On Embassy Row he stood and looked from a distance at the piece of Soviet territory, his expression forlorn. He made as if to go forward, but changed his mind with a shrug.

Apple continued to prowl. All in all, he played spy to his heart's content.

That night Apple read himself to sleep. It was tiredness from the hours of walking that finally made his eyelids droop, not the reading matter. He had become intrigued with parapsychology.

Apple got up early, ate, dressed and went out to the Sunday silence. His intention was to take another prowl, go where all the sightseers gathered, until it was time to call Angus Watkin. And he still needed to think of how he would "find" the group.

Apple was nearing Piccadilly Circus when he became aware of the obvious tail. The same presence had been behind him for some minutes, though it was sensed more than seen, for here the pedestrians were becoming numerous.

Apple went faster, rounded a huddle of people, sagged at the knees and dodged into a shop doorway. Face semi-averted, he watched those who went by.

One took his attention. It was the one who had a determined look on his face, and who, having gone twenty feet on, stopped and began to look all around. There was nothing covert about his manner. He might have been searching anxiously for a lost child.

Apple felt sure he must be mistaken in thinking that this man was a hound. Either he himself was not the hare, or the hound wanted him for something unconnected with the present situation. No operative would act this way. Yet there was the fact of the man's appearance.

He looked as if he had just come down the Steppes. Over six feet tall, deep in the chest, he wore boots and a tieless shirt, and a shoddy suit that was thirty years out of style. His bullet head was shaven, his face round and tough and lumpy. He had the eyes of a subnormal ox.

Still, Apple thought, it had to be a mistake. If he was the hare, it was because the hound thought he was somebody else, having seen him only from the back.

Apple stepped out of the doorway. The man saw him at once. His dull eyes widened, he came bustling forward. It was not so much a matter of following, it seemed; more one of reaching.

Apple, unnerved not only by this strangeness, but also by the patent menace in the hound's attitude, turned away sharply and pushed through people.

He marched to a corner. As he turned it into a side street, he glanced behind. The hound was coming at speed, his face grim, his big arms stiffly swinging. He was the epitome of brute force set on a course of destruction.

So much so, in fact, that Apple wondered if it wasn't an exaggeration. But he took no consolation from that, mainly on account of it being without reason. He went along the side street at a loping stride.

A cafe lay ahead. Apple reached it quickly, went in and wended between the crowded tables. People stared.

There was a door at the rear, but when he had almost got there it became blocked to him by customers. The hound had come in and was approaching.

Apple changed course. He circled back toward the entrance. He glanced back at a crash. The hound had sent a table and its contents flying.

Apple gained the street. Assuring himself that his actions were the natural ones of an innocent, he started running. He went faster as he heard from behind footfalls as rapid as his own.

He was grateful for his long legs. He was amazed by what was happening. People looked at him and he felt absurd, but not absurd enough to stop.

Swinging into the mouth of an alley, he raced on. Two yards separated the buildings on either side, all Sunday dead. Echo racketed the pair of footfalls back and forth.

The alley made an elbow. Apple took it—and was brought to a running halt. He had reached a dead-end. The one door he had time to try was locked. He turned.

The hound arrived. He wasn't even breathing heavily. Moving forward slowly, he said in the grunt-Russian of a Collective, "You, you're called Porter."

Apple tried a smile. "That's right, Comrade. I'm thankful you're not the person I thought you were. I owe him money."

The hound stopped three feet away. He accused in a low, hard voice, "You've been bothering my fiancée."

Apple gaped. "What?"

"You heard me. You know what I mean."

"No I don't."

"You've been trying to steal Olga. You ought not to have done that."

"But she isn't engaged," Apple said. He was stunned with surprise. "She said so."

"Olga pretends a lot," the hound said. His fists were clenched. "But that doesn't matter. I love her. She's promised to me. She's mine."

"This must be a joke," Apple said. With that, Jim Donald's need of an angle flew into his mind. "It is. It's a put-up job. Stop being stupid. I know what you're up to. It's no—"

The punch, swinging upward, caught him on the point of the chin. His head shot up. He went staggering backwards and hit the wall heavily.

The man came charging in. His ox eyes blazed, his teeth were bared. This, Apple knew for sure, was no reporter's gimmick. It was in deadly earnest.

Apple met the rush while being given opposing orders by two instincts. One said he shouldn't fight as a pro because of his cover. The other was the instinct for self-preservation. It won. But aim was damaged by the confusion of orders.

His chop missed the collarbone, his two extended fingers got the hairline instead of the eye. Himself, he took a blow in the ribs and a clout across the face.

The man was fighting like a farmer. He showed no hint of finesse. That put Apple's logic-orientated instinct into control. He was glad those first tries had gone askew.

Three more wild blows from the hound landed on Apple's ribs and face. There were double that number that went wide or became pushes.

Apple fought back. But he was outmatched in this kind of bout. He lacked the weight and solidity, as well as the knowledge of the back yard scrapper. Worse, the height and reach that would have given him the advantage in boxing were liabilities in this scrimmage.

Therefore he went on taking punishment while holding back the blows with which he could easily have crippled or killed the hound.

The side of Apple's face exploded in pain. Next, the other side. His nose and lips followed. His eyes glazed with tears and dizziness. Purblinded, he went on swinging useless punches.

Pain began to take the light away. Before it went completely, in an undulating fashion that Apple found quite interesting, he heard a voice say, "Stay clear of her after this."

He came back the way he had left, to pain and to a voice. They were both his. He was groaning. He opened his eyes and saw sky. Some seconds passed before he recalled where he was and what had happened.

Shock came. In its refusal to believe, it dulled a good deal of the pain. Apple rolled over, got to his hands and knees, stood slowly from there, noting on the way the blood on his shirt and suit.

Getting out a handkerchief, he dabbed cautiously at his face. It was swollen, and in places numb. Blood was coming from his nose and his left eyebrow. He looked at the handkerchief and felt sick.

Walking gave him problems at first. It was like being drunk; limbs refusing to do what they're told. He wanted to lie down and go to sleep. His ribs ached with every step. But he kept going and reached the mouth of the alley.

Two passing women started nervously. They hurried on with backward glances of accusation. Apple lurched across the road. He was walking better, though with stiffer movements. A cruising cab ignored his wave.

Apple entered the narrow streets of Soho. They were as good as deserted. This, the contrast to their workday bustle and cram, added a surrealistic frame to Apple's shock. Everything struck him as incredible.

Dabbing at blood and taking long, taut strides, Apple zagged his way across Soho. He came out on Oxford Street, also a ghost of its usual self, although it had a trickle of traffic. There were taxies, which Apple let go on by: he was nearly home now.

When he did get to the house, he had to fumble to find his key. In the downstairs hallway he let himself sink gratefully to the tiles. He sat there for ten minutes. He would have stayed longer except for hearing sounds of approach from outside. Stiffer yet because of the rest, he went upstairs and into his apartment.

He put on the kettle, turned on the bath taps, stripped to the skin and eased into his consolation robe. Reluctantly, he looked in a mirror. He was a mess.

The blood-streaked face was swollen everywhere, with extra fullness on his top lip, across his nose and around his left eye, which was almost closed. There was a cut in his right eyebrow.

Groaning helped, Apple found, as did the hot, sweet tea; and lowering himself into the steaming bath filled slopover deep was a gift. He lay with his head resting back, repeatedly emptying a sponge over his face. He gave faint groans.

Half an hour later, shock had gone and Apple felt worse. The pain was back in his face and ribs. Elsewhere, rarely used muscles were aching a complaint at having been put to work after their long sleep.

Robe on, Apple limped stiffly around the flat, getting aspirins, putting antiseptic on the cut (long but not deep), avoiding mirrors and finding cigarettes. He lay on the couch and smoked.

He thought about it.

First, could the hound be genuine? He was certainly a Russian, and more likely than not if checks were made it would turn out that news of the flirtation with Olga had reached the Soviet Union, that the hound had arrived that morning from Moscow, and that he had at some time or another dated Olga Goliski.

Genuine he could be, just about, but the stage-dressing was a little too heavy: the clothes, the manner, the way he had found the hare, the rough-and-tumble way of fighting. These seemed to be for the purpose of proving that he wasn't a Hammer. But they were so obvious that a pro wouldn't have been taken in.

Interesting, Apple mused.

He was reaching for another cigarette when the squawk-box buzzed. Sighing, he got up and went to the flat door. He pressed the button. "Hello?"

A static-distorted voice said, "Porter? Hi. Harry Wall here. I got your address from the phone book."

"I'm afraid I'm busy at the moment."

"Aw, come on. The pubs're open. Let's have a couple of jars and talk things over. Or if you like, I'll come up."

"Neither one. Sorry."

The South African asked, "You all right?"

"Perfectly," Apple said. Talking hurt his swollen lip. "There's someone here I'm entertaining. A young lady. You know how it is."

"Sure, sure. But listen. I think you'll be interested in

hearing that our Russian mates have flown the coop. No one's saying where they've gone."

"Curious," Apple said. "Thanks for letting me know. But I must go. So long."

Back on the couch, smoking, Apple set aside the possible involvement in the innings of Harry Wall in favour of the bigger questions.

He began again at the beginning and went over everything carefully. He was particularly impressed with the trouble the KGB had gone to to show that the hound was not of their calling; puzzled by the fact that they surely must have realised that a pro would see through the charade.

Ergo, Apple thought: the KGB had cleared him, because of the burglary and other factors. They believed him to be an innocent. They had tried to give him a scare by having him beaten up. They wanted him out of the way.

Apple sat up slowly. He said aloud, "They want me out of the way because I'm *not* an agent?"

Calling Angus Watkin to get the Russians' whereabouts was no longer feasible, since he was in no condition to go out. Apple forgot that angle. He gave up the rest of the day to thinking, reading, resting and generally pampering himself. Several times he bathed for the stiffness. He had a Chinese meal sent in. He fixed toast with lemon marmalade. He hummed cheerfully.

He toyed with the matter of how he was going to get up to Edinburgh. Plane or train or car? A train appealed strongest, with its suggestion of the Orient Express, spies and intrigue. The shape he was in, however, wouldn't be helped by a long journey by rail, and it made him irritable when people shouted, "Porter!" Driving a car would be a greater sap on his strength. Flying was the best.

Apple enjoyed the indecision and left the question open.

He went to bed at nine o'clock and slept for eleven hours. There was no pain when he awoke.

After breakfast, Apple bundled together two suits, one dirty from his climb into Batewell Hall, one bloody from the fight. He went out. To hide from neighbours his battered face, which had reached its apex in swollenness and hue—yellows and blues—he wore a raincoat with the collar turned up and a hat with the brim flipped low. There were no official observers outdoors, he felt.

In the dry-cleaning shop, the woman pinned tickets on the suits and turned to a pad. She asked, "Name, please?"

Apple was surprised, as well as a little hurt. He had been coming here for years. He said, "Porter."

The woman raised her head, leaned forward, peered. "Why, so you are," she said. "What's happened? I never would have known you, Mr. Porter."

Apple walked home deep in thought.

It took him an hour to get himself fixed up. He wondered how he could ever have believed in Nick Carter. His face he left completely alone; it had its own disguise. Clothes were the problem. He tried on every garment he owned. At last he was satisfied.

Recalling from Training Three that the hairline and neck were focal points, Apple had put on two roll-neck sweaters, the bottom one bulky. Beneath that was a track suit. He had put on a shirt and a windcheater and two pairs of pants. He looked heavier by fifty pounds, which his face couldn't give the lie to because of the swelling.

Height he had fractionally reduced by donning a pair of old heel-less sneakers.

Carrying an overnight bag, which might contain a boxer's gear, he looked like an over-the-hiller on his way to his next defeat.

Apple was generous about giving all credit for the idea of disguise to the woman in the dry-cleaning shop. What he didn't give was much thought to whether or not a disguise was essential, or even desirable. He was enjoying it too much for that. But he did decide against going north by train with everyone else. A passenger with a battered face would be too good a coincidence, as far as the KGB were concerned, whereas they would think nothing of it if they saw him elsewhere, casually.

But there was still the problem of colouring.

When Apple closed the flat door behind him, he had a reservation on the noon plane for Edinburgh. He also had a room booked at the Hotel Anvil. There, inspiration had told him, he could test his appearance on the four lower orders, one of whom was sure to be a KGB who was sure to have seen him at Batewell Hall or the Oceansea. Both reservations were in the name of Albert Mooney.

Below, Apple turned back behind the stairs. He went to the rear door and let himself quietly out. While fairly certain that the house was not being watched, as he had been cleared, he was not about to take any chances.

He crossed the yard, went along an alley, paused at the exit to a street. The way seemed free. He stepped out and began walking in a slouch, his legs shuffling. He had no worry about forgetfully slipping into his normal manner of walking. The shuffle was easier on his lingering stiffness.

A mile from home he came into a humble shopping district. It had all the usual representatives, including a beauty parlour. The place was small and smelled of singed hair. Two young women looked up from being their own manicurists.

Apple asked in a rough voice, "You do dye jobs here?"

The women nodded, said, "Yes."

"Black?"

"Any colour your wife wants," one of the women said. "Green if she wants."

Apple shook his head. "It's for me, not the wife. I'm trying to get away from her. It's a disguise, see. So you can give me a black job on eyebrows and hair after you've chopped me down to a crew-cut. Okay?"

No one paid much attention to Albert Mooney on his way out to Heathrow Airport on an Underground train. People tend to avoid failure. The face, in any event, was unattractive with its patches of sick colour.

At the airport Apple bought his ticket, checked in and went to the departure lounge. Most of the thirty-odd passengers were clustered around the bar. As he shuffled there himself, Apple picked out several faces that seemed familiar to him, though he could put an identity with only one: the man who didn't want anyone to forget Hungary. He was talking passionately in French to a man in soldier's uniform. Passing by that way, Apple learned that the topic was football.

He got a beer and leaned back on the counter. Again, Albert Mooney drew scant attention; and when Jim Donald came into the lounge his professional glance that took in everyone failed to quicken with recognition.

The flight was announced. Not forgetting to drain every last drop of his beer, as an Albert Mooney would,

Apple went with the others to the door. He worked along the queue until he was standing next to the reporter.

Jim Donald glanced up, turned away, turned back for a longer look. He said, "Hey."

"Huh?"

"Been in the wars, haven't you, old son?"

Apple ran a hand from back to front over his short-cropped hair. "So what?"

The reporter shrugged and changed places. Apple allowed himself a smile of satisfaction and pride.

Shuffling along an endless-seeming corridor to the plane, Apple thought back over his other recent actions, checking that they were as sound as the disguise.

He had been right, he assured himself, in not reporting his scene with the hound to the police, making a charge of assault; in respect of cover, it could be seen as a case of protesting too much. The motive he had given in the beauty parlour for the clip and dye job was awful enough to be convincing; the elaborations of a pro might have given the women the idea that their client was on the run, a crook or escaped convict or murder suspect; the police being called would have been awkward in respect of delay. Telling the dry-cleaner that he had been attacked by two muggers was okay; no man will relate how he got bested in a fight.

On the plane Apple found himself sitting beside a girl in her early twenties. She was silent and tense until they were clear of the ground, when, without preamble, she began to pour out her enthusiasm for the Russian dance troupe. She had seen it every night in London, would see it in Edinburgh (after being at the airport to join in the welcome), and planned to see it again in Dublin. Apple finally cut her off by closing his eyes. Albert Mooney didn't give a stuff about dancing.

The forty-minute ride passed quickly. Outside the air-port, in the jumble of arrivers and greeters, Apple claimed a taxi. He got in and asked to be taken first to wherever it was that the Russian mind-readers were appearing.

"Never heard of 'em," the driver said. "Hold on." He leaned out of his window and bawled the question to an-other cabbie.

Apple cringed. He realised with dreariness how easily the cleverest and most complex of plans could be massa-cred. But he didn't look around to see if anyone was finding Albert Mooney's destination curious.

Informed, the driver steered away. He said defensively that a person couldn't be expected to know everything. Albert Mooney asked where were all the men in skirts he'd heard they had up here in Scotland. He was ignored.

They drove through the austerely beautiful streets of Edinburgh. From ground to overcast sky, the pervading colour was grey. The pedestrians looked as if they pre-ferred to laugh with their mouths closed, but doubted if they would find anything to laugh about.

A poster outside the lecture hall announced that the Hibernian Psychic League was playing host to para-psychologists from seven different countries. Plastered sternly over that was a banner saying SOLD OUT.

"Hotel Anvil," Apple said. He was unconcerned by the lack of tickets. He wasn't even sure that he would be going to the performance. One thing he did know: in his condition, he wasn't about to do any climbing.

He felt better without a plan.

The hotel was on a quiet road and its sign was meek. Apple went into a plant-choked lobby no bigger than his living room. Behind the desk stood a small, gnarled man wearing morning dress. He was polite.

Formalities over, Apple asked, "This isn't where the Russian dancers're staying, is it?"

The man shook his head. He explained about the two groups, and the smaller one's division, adding, "Our four are due in half an hour or so."

Apple shrugged Albert Mooney's disinterest. "Just so long as nobody starts doing the Cossack jig near my room."

"You're in a single at the back, sir. Nice and quiet. The others will be up on five. You won't be disturbed."

The information had come so easily, the clerk might have been paid to give it; but, Apple mused, only a pro would suspect that he had.

When Apple got to his room, after climbing two flights of stairs, he felt exhausted. At the hand-basin he splashed water on his face, which he then examined in the mirror. The swelling was holding well. The blues were turning black, the yellows had a greenish tinge. He was surprised the clerk had granted him admission.

Apple lay on the bed, which, Presbyterianly, was narrower than the normal single. He looked at his watch. He told himself he would rest for fifteen minutes before going down to see and be seen by the four equal serfs.

He fell asleep.

Two hours later, Apple tried to turn over. His arm went on sinking through space. Alarm jerked him stark awake, but not in time for him to keep from rolling off the bed.

He landed with a thud that roused his every resentful muscle. He lay still, feeling wretched, until the pain faded, at which point he saw the absurdity of the happening. He laughed. He laughed the louder because of his thankfulness a moment ago that no one could see him now.

Apple sobered on looking at the time. The Russian check-in was past. He got up and smoked a cigarette. After that he shaved; his ginger beard was beginning to show—an odd contrast to the black hair.

He left the room. Although there was no one to be seen, the hotel hummed with life, the afternoon activity of arrival and settle-in. It was like being surrounded by invisible people.

Apple went up the flights of stairs slowly. He didn't want to exhaust himself again. His extra clothing, he knew, must weigh a good fifteen pounds. He was glad of the cool weather.

As Apple turned onto the fifth floor, he saw Olga.

He froze in surprise.

The girl didn't even glance at him. She finished closing the door behind her, rattling the handle to make sure the lock had caught, then went along the passage in the other direction. She wore a robe, a shower-cap, and carried a washbag. She turned in at a door marked Bath.

Apple slowly let his muscles relax. He moved to a lean on the wall. Once his surprise had eased, he thought about it.

She could be here in case that thick innocent Appleton Porter refused to take a hint, or was so much in love that he couldn't help himself. Relegation to semi-isolation and lesser luxury may be a form of punishment for playing along with the same admirer. It could be that each one of the team had to take a turn away from the pack for some reason. She might have gone into one of those sombre Russian moods that demanded solitude (she had, he recalled, looked unusually straight-faced). Olga being here had many possible and natural explanations.

So why was he beginning to feel tense?

Apple straightened. He backed away onto the staircase, turned and went on down. His mind was busy, though only with the self-reprimand that he was acting through emotion, not logic. But that, of course, was why he had been given this job.

He remembered to shuffle on reaching the lobby. Half a dozen people were checking in. Apple went by and outside. Deciding to hell with his shuffle, he began to stride along the street. He even enjoyed the twinges of pain.

There was faint hope of a passing taxi, Apple knew. Cabs didn't rove for trade anywhere but London. He would have to ride shanks' pony. He wondered grumpily where that stupid expression came from.

His enjoyment of the pain ended when, taken by urgency, he started a loping run. His body, ribs in particular, yammered at him to stop. He did, but only because a look at his watch told him he would make it in time. If, that is, his strength held out.

Apple had passed the bicycle before its presence had registered on his consciousness. He stopped and looked back. There was no one near, and no one to be seen through the windows of the house against whose wall the bicycle rested.

Apple didn't think about it. The next moment he was pedalling along the street. The expected shout of outrage didn't come. He turned a corner and set his lungs to breathing again. He was firm with himself in not musing pityingly about the owner.

Soon he was in traffic, wobbling along like the beginner he almost was. He hadn't cycled for years. But his legs spun without effort, his pains were dormant, and the fact of the theft gave him a pleasurable tingle of guilt—though that was in the shadow of his urgency.

Just when he thought he was near his goal, he realised he had taken a wrong turning. He was lost.

The man he asked for directions, a senior citizen, was lonely. He began giving snippets of information on the buildings Apple would pass, if he got the way right. Apple kept lying, "Yes yes, I know." Every ten seconds he looked at his watch. It had never had such attention as today.

Finally he could stand the suspense no longer. "Sorry," he said, in truth, and pushing off, took a running leap into the saddle. He pedalled furiously, got on the right track, and arrived at the railway station with five minutes to spare.

The bicycle he left leaning on a lamp-post by the entrance. He went inside, shuffling. There were scores of people present under the high, echoing roof. Most were travellers or greeters. Some were there on account of the Russians.

A group carried a banner that bid a welcome from the Soviet-Scotia Friendship Club. Nearby stood the Hungary man with his placard; he was reading a book. There were policemen. There were two obvious Hammers. The obligatory bouquet-carrying child in party dress looked as if she needed to go to the bathroom. Two reporters waited by the closed door of the bar.

Apple took everything in while making an aimless circle of the concourse. He had a cigarette dangling from a corner of his thick lips. He watched Jim Donald arrive, go to the camera-laden newsmen and introduce himself.

Loudspeakers gave out what sounded like information.

Greeters of all persuasions started edging forward toward the railings that separated the concourse from the tracks. The little girl was hustled away.

Apple positioned himself at the railings, six feet from the gate that was the centre of attention. He was soon surrounded by others. He sagged a little at the knees.

Beyond the rails, along the platform, waited an official greeting body—probably, Apple thought, Soviet consular people, though at junior level; bigger guns would be at the airport to meet the dancers. He wondered if the little girl would make it back in time.

The train bullied in and came to an angry, throbbing halt. More people crowded forward. The passengers began to alight. One of the first to come to the gate and through was Harry Wall, his jazzy-coloured clothes as apt as a scream in a cloister.

Other travellers streamed through. When they had thinned to a trickle, the visiting Russians could be seen on the platform, gathered together near the consular people.

In the group was Olga.

Apple watched. His eyes were steady, his mind was still. He watched to be sure. He watched until the two groups started to move toward the gate.

Turning, he sidled away through the crowd.

His urgency came back as he passed outside under the entry arch. He had forgotten the existence of his stolen bicycle. It could not, in any case, be seen now, for the area had become busy. People were milling around among luggage and taxies.

Apple was unaware of his roughness as he pushed through to the outer edge of the crowd, where he was successful in beating an old lady to a cab.

He slammed inside. "Hotel Anvil," he said tersely.

"Right you are, sir."

"Fast if you want to double your fare."

The driver did. He sped away, jumped two sets of traffic lights, cut around other cars as if he were made of rubber, and pulled up outside the hotel with a squeal of brakes.

Apple thrust him more than the promise. He got out and strode into the Anvil. Guests were still being checked in. Apple went to the stairs and ran up.

Panting, he came to the fifth floor. He went to the room he had seen Olga come out of. He knocked firmly. After a lapse of some seconds a female voice asked, in stilted English:

"Yes, what is it?"

"Telegram for you," Apple said.

"One moment, please."

"Of course." He stared at the door.

It receded. Standing there was the spokeswoman for the mind-reading team, in her boots and trouser suit. She adjusted her blue-tinted spectacles.

"You have a telegram?"

"Yes, for Mrs. Watson."

The spokeswoman shook her head. "You have the wrong room. Sorry." She closed him out.

Apple stared on at the door. Twins, he thought.

FOUR

Apple came out of the pub. He had gone in a minute ago to sit with a drink, but while waiting to be served had found he preferred to be moving. He had left.

Like a conjuring trick, he thought, it was obvious when you knew how it worked. So much so that you were surprised you hadn't figured it out for yourself. And this one worked because it was kept simple. The change in appearance was done through camouflage, not direct disguise. Apart from the blue-tinted glasses, there were no facial aids that could fail or rouse suspicion.

It was the overall picture that was so radically different, Apple mused as he walked. Olga was her natural self, small in flat-heeled shoes, slim in waisted dresses. Her hair was flat to her head, drawn back into the bun. The Sister was several inches taller in her boots, heavier because of the padding under the trouser suit, larger in cranium on account of the loose hair—which was drawn forward to blur that important hairline.

The twins travelled separately and stayed in different hotels. They were near to one another only when on a stage, and then for no more than half an hour, and with company. The whole thing was simple and effective. It would probably have been foolproof against a pro, but had been put at risk in a Fools-rush.

Apple smiled at his ownership of knowledge. That he

had come by it through semi-blunder rather than clev-
erness was beside the point. He knew what only a hand-
ful in this country did—the other three at the Anvil, Kutuzov and friends, higher people at the embassy; the
manipulators. Certainly the rest of the team were in the
dark. And did Olga know the full extent of what was happening?

A passer-by stopped Apple to ask the way to Princess
Street. Apple was able to oblige. The next moment he
asked for directions himself, from a postman. He headed
for the Black Gordon Hotel. He was keeping to his
shuffle.

Apple wondered what would be in the next box to be
opened. The mind-reading act was a bafflement. Inside
that lay a mystery. That had its own secret. The secret
had a further puzzle, which held the last enigma.

A game, he thought.

Turning a corner, Apple came onto a broad, gracious
avenue. The buildings were sturdy Victorians with pil-
lared porticoes. Midway along the street stood a crowd.

It was across the way from the Black Gordon, Apple
saw as he drew closer. He also saw the expected faces.
Even though the crowd looked placid, there were policemen fronting the hotel. The Scots took no chances. Their
carefulness went beyond small coins.

Apple stayed at a distance. For the duration of a cigarette, he watched. Harry Wall left and strolled to a
nearby pub. The Hungary-reminder read his book steadily. The police warned a man who had ventured to the
centre of the roadway. Jim Donald gave a yawn.

Apple retraced his steps. The urgency which had been
with him earlier was still present, though in lesser degree,
like the difference in his body pains when he ran or

walked. But he didn't know what his next move should be.

He was diverted from thinking about it by a child whizzing by on a tricycle. He quickened his shuffle. There was quite a way to go. He was glad to have a goal.

When Apple got there, to the railway station entrance, he was relieved to see that the bicycle was still where he had left it. He had been worried about thieves.

Unnoticed by anyone, he wheeled the machine to the road, mounted and cycled off. He condoned the niceness of his intentions by pointing out to himself that this would never occur to a pro. He was acting correctly.

Apple found the right street without any trouble, yet wasn't sure about the house. He cycled back and forth slowly. The problem was solved by a man who dashed into his path with widespread arms, shouting, "Got you, got you!"

Apple stopped and dismounted. The man continued to hold his arms up at the sides. He was short and wiry, forty, and had frizzy hair that stood out from a bald pate. He twitched his anger.

"Yes," he said. "Got you."

Apple, still acting correctly, gave an apologetic smile with, "Sorry about this. I borrowed the bike to get to the station. I was in a terrible hurry. A panic. I had to get there fast."

"That," the man said, "you can explain to the sergeant at the police station."

"If you wish. But as you can see, I was bringing it back to where I found it."

"I've heard that one before."

"Anyway, I'd like to thank you for the bike's existence,"

Apple said calmly. "You'll never know how much it helped me."

The man sighed. He lowered his arms, one of which he then swung in a gesture of dismissal. The change might have been due to Apple's story and manner, or Albert Mooney's height, bulk and battered face. Whichever, the man made no more mention of police as he grumbled about people who didn't respect the property of others and . . .

A minute later Apple was walking alone along the street. The truth, he thought, that's what had turned the trick. Playing it straight.

Which gave him what he had been looking for: his next move. After all, he was still supposedly trying to contact a defector, something he had forgotten about.

He quickened his shuffle and went in search of a telephone. The booth he found had half its small-pane windows broken. He didn't feel the need to hold the door ajar as he made his call to the Black Gordon Hotel.

Apple told the switchboard that he was the Russian vice-consul in Edinburgh. He wanted to speak with Miss Olga Goliski. There was no hindrance. Clearly, that nuisance Appleton Porter had been written off.

"Hello?" a voice said in Russian.

"Hello, Olga. This is Appleton."

"Oh, how nice. Are you calling from London?"

Apple didn't know what would be the best answer to that one. He said, "Can you hear me? This is a bad line. Can you talk? Are you alone?"

"I can hear you very well, Appleton. The line's all right at this end. Natasha's here."

"I wonder if you know that I met your fiancé."

Olga said, "My what?"

Apple explained, describing the man in full but the incident only in part. They had argued, not fought. Olga sounded incredulous. Apple decided she wasn't that good an actress.

_ "By the description," Olga said, "he could have been one of several friends. But I'm not engaged to anyone. How fantastic. I can't believe it."

Apple let her go on in similar vein for a while before plunging in with, "Have you thought about freedom?"

After a pause, Olga said, "I can't say."

"Ask Natasha to go for a walk."

"She's already left the room. She's very polite. I didn't mean I couldn't say because of Natasha. It's that I don't know if I've thought about it or not. You sound very mysterious."

Apple tacked by asking, "When are you due to appear onstage at the theatre?"

"In about an hour. Ours is the first turn tonight. We'll leave the hotel at the last minute, as always. I have plenty of time to talk to you."

Apple said, "I want you to think about freedom in the next sixty minutes. Just think about it. Politics apart."

"I hate politics. Fashions are so much nicer. It's a pity we don't have the same taste, you and I."

"But we do, Olga," Apple said. "I'm a sterner critic than you, that's all."

Using the protective plural, the girl asked, "When are we going to see you again?"

"Soon. Very soon."

"Are you in London?"

Apple raised his voice. "Hello? Are you there? The line's getting worse. I can't—" He cut himself off by depressing the cradle.

Staying well away from both hotels, Apple went in search of a cafe. He knew that Edinburgh was unique among the world's capital cities in that it had no night clubs, few restaurants and a scarcity of casual eating houses (knowledgeable visitors to the Festival took their own sandwiches).

This dearth was fine with Apple. The search would serve the same purpose as the following meal, for which he had no appetite: a phony filler of time. Waiting with nothing to do made Apple edgy. He preferred having some task to get through while worrying that he was going to be late.

Since asking could have spoiled things—there might have been a place right around the corner—Apple shuffled quickly along street after street. They were busy with commuters. Lamps were on against the gathering dusk.

A shabby man approached Apple and asked for the price of a drink. If Apple hadn't remembered that begging was legal in Scotland, he would have been suspicious. He winced as Albert Mooney said tartly that he was a poor man himself.

Apple came to an ice-cream parlour, which, like a thousand others north of the border, was Italian-owned. The woman serving said in broken Scottish that she could manage beans on toast, if that would do.

It would, with an ice cream starter so he wouldn't be left waiting empty-handed. Through the cone and the gooey snack, both eaten languidly, Apple worried about being late.

Paying, he hurried out. The streets were dark where the lamplight failed to reach. Apple allowed himself to let the shuffle go—until he came within sight of the lecture hall.

There was no one standing out front, though four policemen sat in one of the many parked cars. The officers
looked at him bleakly as he shuffled into the lobby.

Its sole occupant was a man in usher's uniform. In the
tones of authority Apple asked him, "Everything all
right?"

"Er—yes."

"No signs of trouble?"

"Well, no."

"Don't forget, if a problem comes up, we're right outside." He nodded and went on to swing doors, slipped
through them and was in the dim auditorium.

Apple's timing was excellent. The team members were
settling on their chairs, the spokeswoman was coming to
the front of the stage to give her spiel.

Behind the seating near Apple stood several people. He
joined them quietly. He was hoping the usher would stay
bluffed; at least for ten minutes.

The Sister seemed to take longer with her speech tonight, though Apple realised that could be the doing of
his own nerves. Olga was looking at the floor pensively.
Beside her, Natasha was drumming her fingers on her
heavy thighs. Below, on the front row, Kutuzov sat in his
usual twisted position.

From the corners of his eyes, Apple looked at the people standing near him. The one right at his side was a
Hammer. Apple sagged at the knees. He looked the other
way at a glimpse of light. The swing doors had opened,
admitting the usher. He stood peering around.

Apple moved away. He went softly down the centre
aisle. A dozen rows from the front, he crouched beside a
seat. The occupant, a woman, stared at him.

He whispered, "Could I see your ticket, please?"

The Sister was plodding toward the end of her speech. The woman beside Apple asked, "What on earth do you mean?"

Someone went, "Shhh."

Apple said, "Your ticket, please, madam."

"Who are you?"

"Ticket, please."

A man leaned past the woman, asking, "What does the fellow want, dear?"

The someone went, "Shhh."

The woman said, "Shush, yourself."

Up on the stage, the Sister quickened her pace to bring the speech to a close—probably, Apple thought, because of mistaking the sounds from below as audience boredom.

The woman said to Apple, "Go away, whoever you are."

The man with her asked, "Is the fellow bothering you, dear?"

Above, the spokeswoman said, "Now I would like to ask for a volunteer from the audience."

Apple shot erect. He marched to the front and strode up a middle stairway to the stage.

The team looked at him with interest but no recognition. The Sister showed both, though the former was barbed. Her eyes said, What is he doing here, the same man who came to the wrong door with a telegram?

The eyes went to the man with the silver teeth, came back to Apple as he shuffled forward with his hand out. The shake was as brief as the Sister's smile. She took him by the arm and turned him to face the audience. Her hold continued.

Apple realised the point of that. He remembered that the spokeswoman always stood beside the subject with a hand on top of the chair, but she was also touching the person's shoulder, a contact to help in mind-reading. She had done the same with him when he had been the subject.

The Sister was watching him closely, her face set. Apple thought with care; using English:

Does she suspect?

The woman blinked, stared on.

Apple thought, *Delay. That's important. Delay. Stretch it out as long as possible.*

The Sister's eyes roved his face. Her grip on his arm was tight and rigid.

From the audience came murmurs and shuffling. The man with the silver teeth was leaning forward in his seat, one finger pressed to his wart.

Still using English, because the artificiality of the matter would be less apparent to someone not perfect in the language, Apple thought:

But they don't seem worried about the dancers.

The woman stiffened. She was waiting for more. Apple, however, dared go no further than that vagueness. In a Scots accent he asked pleasantly, "Well, what do I do, miss?"

She let go of his arm and stood back. "Tell the audience about yourself," she said, with a glance at the front row. Turning away, she strode across the stage and into the wings.

Kutuzov got up smartly. He went up the aisle and through a doorway. The Hammer from the back was already moving down to follow. The audience was hissing its puzzlement.

Apple swung around the other way. The team looked bewildered. The two female members were staring at Albert Mooney with expressions of doubt, as though they were approaching the brink of the truth.

Apple went over. He took Olga by the hand and pulled her to her feet. He said, "Let's go."

The others rose as well. The leader with the white moustache asked, "What's all this?"

Natasha pointed. "Why, it's—it's—"

Apple yanked Olga away. Towing her behind him he ran off the stage—the opposite side from that taken by the Sister. He dodged around flies, came to the backdrop.

Olga kept gasping, "Wait."

"Not yet. I'll explain outside."

"Outside?"

"Keep moving."

"I know that voice," Olga said. "You're Appleton." It was half question, half statement.

"Yes. Come on."

"I don't know," she said, trying to hang back.

Apple tugged her on, holding tightly to her hand. They came to the end of the first backdrop, where Apple stopped, despite the sounds of pursuit from behind.

Ahead, in the backstage area, the Sister and Kutuzov and others were clustered by a telephone. They didn't look around. But the stage-door was out as an exit.

Apple slipped behind another backdrop, ran to its end, headed away from the stage into a dimness of flotsam and clutter. When Olga protested again he said:

"Think fashion. Think clothes."

There were still sounds of chase. Apple motioned to Olga to follow his example as he began to move softly, slowing to a walk. They went past hunks of ancient scenery, stacks of chairs, a variety of lecterns.

They arrived at a wall. It was so dark now that Apple

had to feel his way along the brickwork. His hand met metal, slid down and found a bar. He pushed. Night air rushed in through the opening door.

Apple led Olga out to a street.

"I can't *do* this," she said. "Stop."

"You're already doing it. Keep moving."

"I don't know what's going on."

"Escape, that's what."

"This is insane."

"Right," Apple said.

They were running along the street, side by side. Holding the girl's elbow, Apple was pulling as much as pushing. He cursed his big mistake in not having hired a car.

That, he thought, would have looked so much better.

From behind came the crash of opening doors, a stammer of footfalls, voices.

Crouching, Apple pushed Olga between two parked cars to the roadway. They continued running. A truck flashed its lights at them as it went past.

Olga panted, "You're forcing me to do this." She sounded relieved. "Yes, you are."

Apple accused, "You haven't been thinking freedom."

"I don't know what you mean. Free? I am free. There are no slaves in the Soviet Union."

A fast glance behind showed Apple a group of figures. They were running in the roadway some fifty yards back. He gasped, "Russia is a prison."

"You people in the West have strange ideas," Olga said. "Where are we *going?*"

"I haven't a clue."

"What?"

Apple was trying to recall from Training Seven how to

get into and start a car without keys. His mind in that direction was a blank, which, he realised, was just as well for an innocent. He wondered if the people behind had guns.

"Tell the truth," he said. "You have been thinking about living in the West, haven't you?"

"Are you wearing a mask?"

"You've been seeing yourself going into a shop and buying a dress that's fashionable right now, today."

Olga panted, "Who wouldn't?"

They came to a junction. Apple pushed Olga across it obliquely. Behind them a horn gave a tinny beep. Apple stopped and turned. He put himself directly in the path of the approaching car.

It was an antique Fiat, glittering with care, its driver a young man in a deerstalker hat. He brought the relic to a screeching halt.

Apple whipped open the back door. He bundled Olga inside, climbed in himself and snapped, "Hospital! Quick! This is an emergency!"

The driver had turned. He had a thin, intense face like a mountaineer. "What?" he said. "Get oot 'o mah car. Stop talking gibberish."

Apple realised he had spoken in Russian. He said it again in English. The driver faced front and sent the car ambling forward.

"Right y'are," he said. "Be kind enough not to bleed on mah upholstery."

"It's internal," Apple said, looking behind. Only one figure was giving chase, and it quickly faded as the Fiat began to gather cumbersome speed.

The driver asked, "Do you fancy any hospital in particular?"

"Leave that to you. And thanks."

Olga gripped his arm. "I have to go back. This has gone far enough. There'll be terrible trouble. The performance has been ruined."

"The other five can carry on alone."

"No, I must go back." She seemed to doubt it. "The longer I stay away, the worse trouble there'll be."

"My dear girl," Apple said. "You have escaped. This is it. You've skipped the Iron Curtain."

"What's an iron curtain?"

"Never mind. Just get it into your head that as of five minutes ago, your home is here."

Olga said, "But I can't do that."

"Of course you can. People do it all the time."

They braced themselves as the Fiat went around a corner. "Did you see the needle then?" the driver said proudly. "It touched forty."

Apple told him, "Wonderful."

"Wait till we get on a straight bit."

Headlights lit the car's interior, coming from behind. Apple looked back. A limousine was catching up. He turned to the driver to say urgently:

"I think the blood's coming out. Hurry."

Olga said, "I can't stay."

"Worried about never seeing your sister again?"

She shook her head. "We're not close. We don't even like each other very much. We're totally different."

"Was it through her that your fiancé heard about me?" Apple asked. "Did you telephone her in Moscow?"

The girl laughed, stopped laughing, said, "We never call each other. And I have no fiancé."

"So you claim."

"Listen. What happened on the stage tonight? Why did Anna suddenly walk off like that?"

"The spokeswoman?" Apple evaded, noting the growing glare of the headlights.

"Yes. Anna Yudenich."

"Maybe she felt ill."

The driver said, "Forty-three." His voice was tense. "I hope the police're asleep."

Olga touched Apple's face. "It isn't a mask."

"The KGB beat me up."

She gasped, "I don't believe it."

"And they're behind us now."

They both turned to the back window. There was nothing to see except the headlights. Apple said, "So if you're not close to that older sister of yours—what's the hold?"

"Listen. I want to know if the KGB really did this to you."

"No, I just said that. It was your fiancé."

"But—"

They were thrown off balance as the antique car swooped out to pass a truck. When Apple righted himself he saw that they were on a long straight road. There was no traffic ahead.

The driver said a terse, "Forty-eight."

The headlights shifted aside: the limousine was pulling out to pass. Olga sank into a corner of the seat, her back to the big car. Apple told the driver:

"The next turning on this side. See it? My doctor lives down there. Better than a hospital."

The big car came abreast. A Hammer was driving. Passengers were two more Hammers and the man with the silver teeth. Every face was steady but grim.

The Fiat reached the corner. It swerved into the side

street, its tyres yelling. More of the same noise came from
the limousine as it braked.

"On second thought," Apple said, "the hospital's best.
Go straight on."

"Right y'are."

"Drive like the wind."

The man tugged at the peak of his deerstalker. "Aye."

The way ahead was narrow between the parked cars.
Even though the limousine caught up swiftly, it couldn't
pass. But within seconds the Fiat was abruptly back on a
main road, having entered it from an angle.

The driver said excitedly, "Fifty-one!"

Olga asked her hands, "Where would I work?"

With an engine roar and a blast on the horn, the big car
drew alongside. It edged on past, then cut in front and
began to slow.

The young man in the deerstalker hat snarled. As if
holding reins, he leaned back to bring his relic to a shud-
dering, clanking stop.

The other car also stopped. The four men alighted with
efficient speed and came striding back. Kutuzov said,
"Ah, good evening, Mr. Porter."

Those were the last quiet words spoken over the next
two minutes. Jumping out of his Fiat, the driver snatched
off his hat, flung it to the ground and began on a shouted
tirade against the occupants of the other car.

Blinking at the language, Apple got out and drew Olga
after him. They stood opposite the KGBs. The driver was
in between. No one else had a chance to speak.

The two minutes ended when the police arrived.

Drawing to a halt neatly one after the other were a motor-cycle, a patrol car and a Black Maria. Apple stopped counting policemen after six.

What followed was mild chaos with a semblance of order, division into three separate units helping, use of two languages an impediment. While their colleagues watched and frowned and circled, three officers asked questions of the Russians, the driver, Apple and Olga.

With one of the Hammers translating (his English Oxford perfect), Kutuzov and his men politely declined to answer any questions. They showed their passports and claimed diplomatic immunity.

The man in the deerstalker hat was denying that he had been speeding, or that he had been playing races with these foreigners, who, he said, had tried to run him into the side for no reason at all.

Apple told his policeman about hitching a ride with his girl friend in the Fiat, which had never gone over thirty. He looked around for Olga, but found that she had been drawn quietly away by one of the Hammers. She looked at him blankly while being ushered without fuss into the big car.

"What's that?" the policeman asked Apple, taking hold of his bicep. "What's that you say?"

Apple was surprised at the belligerence. "You mean about us hitching a—"

"Look, laddie," the officer said in a loud voice. "You can't say things like that and get away with it."

"What?"

"Been at the bottle, have you? Well, we know how to deal with your sort up here. We don't stand for no nonsense."

Apple said, "I know my rights."

"We'll rights you," the policeman laughed grimly. "Just you come this way, laddie."

Protesting, Apple allowed himself to be led to the Black Maria. He was shoved inside at the back. The door slammed. In semi-darkness he felt his way onto a bench-seat along one side. He heard a voice say:

"That police officer's acting is a shade worse than yours, Porter."

"Good evening, sir."

"But I suppose it did the trick."

"Yes, sir," Apple said. He could barely make out the shape of Angus Watkin, sitting on the opposite side near the front. "May I, with respect, point out that this cop-interference ploy has been already used once in this operation?"

"I was caught unawares," Watkin said shortly. "It was the best I could think of on the spur of the moment."

"And you did have the equipment at hand."

"Quite so."

The van began to move. Apple said, "I wonder why we pronounce it Black Mar-eye-a instead of Mar-ee-a."

"I imagine to avoid offence to the Maria of Ave fame."

"That's reasonable."

Drily: "Thank you."

Apple was reaching in his pocket for cigarettes when he heard himself blurt, "I know I've been on a Fools-rush." He forgot about smoking.

"I should hope so by now," Watkin said. "You're a bright chap, Porter. But you didn't let that get in your way. You've worked out admirably. The opposition believed your cover. That's why you were bashed around."

"I know," Apple said with a crust on his voice. "I was able to figure that one out all by myself."

Angus Watkin folded his arms. "Don't be sarcastic. It doesn't suit you."

"Sorry, sir."

"Anyway, I give you full marks for losing the fight. Also for matching general appearance to beaten-up face. Well done. Your Back-up was flummoxed for a while."

"Would he," Apple said casually, "be a man with a poster asking us not to forget Hungary?" He felt hurt when his superior said:

"It wouldn't be a man at all. It's female."

"Oh."

"Your poster-carrier is a harmless crank who's been around for twenty years. He pickets everything from vivisectionists to cricket games. He likes the outdoor life."

"I thought he had to be straight," Apple lied.

"Your Back-up waved a Russian flag outside the Oceansea, and had to sit beside you on the plane up here to make sure it was you and not Albert Moody."

"Mooney," Apple murmured in quiet spite. He was worried by the fact of being given background information, as well as Angus Watkin having used the past tense a moment ago. It was as if the innings had ended.

Behind the driver was a small, barred window. Through it the lights from passing cars flashed intermittently across Watkin's bland face, illuminating it faintly. Apple was unable to gauge response when he said:

"The twin thing is very neat."

"Very," Watkin said. He could have been bluffing. He would hate to have to admit he didn't know about it.

Apple switched away. "My disguise worked except

with the two girls on the team. They'd seen more of me than the others. It must've been Natasha who told Kutuzov—he greeted me by name just now."

"Is Natasha KGB?"

Apple liked the question, the admission of ignorance, yet it made Watkin's knowledge of there being twins more likely. He said, "I shouldn't think so. Telling who I was could have been a natural act, or she might have done it so they wouldn't get hot and bothered."

"Kutuzov's never been hot in his life."

"The spokeswoman didn't know me," Apple said. He told about the telegram gambit. Angus Watkin commented that it was nice and old-fashioned.

The Black Maria began to slow. It lurched sideways in making a turn, then came to a stop. At the front, doors opened and closed.

Watkin said, "The operation has reached a crucial moment. Now we know what the score is, it's time we helped the Russians get rid of the defector they've been madly trying to push onto someone."

They got out of the van. Apple looked around a dim yard that held two patrol cars, one with a flat tyre. Every window in the nearby building showed light. In one, a policewoman was combing her hair.

Angus Watkin said, "Yes, your face is quite messy."

"They meant business."

"That they did, Porter, and I can understand exactly how they felt."

Apple said, "They were pretty casual tonight."

"They weren't expecting innocent Porter to get very far. If you had been an agent, they would have got rough. They don't want a defection until they're the organisers."

"Of course."

Angus Watkin said, "I may have to pull you out, Porter. They don't want you. They want their prize planted right."

Earnestly, Apple said, "They'll be having second thoughts now. They'll suspect my cover. Especially after this repeated police routine."

"Suspicion isn't enough. They have to be sure, after all the conniving they've gone to."

"All right, sir. We think of some way to let my cover slip."

Angus Watkin put his hands behind his back and strolled away. While watching him anxiously, Apple got out cigarettes and lit up. He lit the wrong end, coughed, started again. He was smoking deeply by the time Watkin came back, asking:

"Do they have the slightest inkling that you know about the twin set-up?"

"No, sir. I'm positive they don't. I doubt if many among their own group know about it."

"You did that thing with the telegram."

"I could have been looking for Olga. I said nothing."

"What was it that Anna picked up from your mind on-stage?"

"I thought they didn't seem to be worried about the dancers. It could be read as a complaint: Why was I having problems when the dance troupe was being feted and meeting people?"

Watkin said, "But she thought it could mean someone was getting at the dancers, right then. It had to be checked."

"Yes. So it casts more doubt on my cover. For all they

know, there might have been a snatch-attempt on the
dancers that never got to the first stage."

Watkin took another short stroll. He looked to have not
a care in the world. He came back and said, "Tell me
about the sisters, as it appears to you."

No longer caring if he was confirming or informing,
Apple said, "They look alike but otherwise it's a case of
chalk and cheese. They have nothing in common. Olga is
sweet, feminine and not very bright. Anna's the hard and
sharp one. She's probably a Party member, maybe also
KGB. She learned English. She went on to develop her
extra-sensory perception beyond what she was born with
—the ESP rapport that's common with twins. She's the
mind-reader. Onstage, she reads the subject's message or
whatever and thinks it over to Olga, who pretends to get
it from the others as well as herself."

Watkin said, "Would you agree that, apart from this
bit of subterfuge, Olga's in the dark as to what's behind
this?"

"Yes, sir, I would. She's the kind who's liable to let secrets slip."

"Good. Go on."

"She, Olga, never progressed from the basic twin-rap-
port stage. Probably not interested. Her thought-trans-
ference is good only with her sister. She'd be useless to us
or anyone else."

Unexpectedly, Angus Watkin asked, "How about a cup
of tea, Porter?"

"Fine, sir."

They went into the building and along a passage that
had a smell of disinfectant. Somewhere below, a voice
was singing drunkenly, while another voice was telling it
to shut up or be strangled. From behind closed doors

came the natter of typewriters, a radio playing jazz, two males laughing.

Watkin led Apple into a canteen. It was bleak. A detective and three uniformed men were playing cards and studiously ignored the newcomers as they served themselves with tea.

When they were settled at a corner table, Angus Watkin said, "I want you to play Soviet Intelligence, please. Now tell me, what are you up to?"

"I want to plant an ear in a foreign secret service," Apple said. "Let's say with you, the British, though any will do. First, I leak stories of a possible defector among the visiting Russians. The next rumour narrows it to the psychics. I hint that one in the team is an outsider, which reverses to be the only real insider, the single mind-reader. With that I give you pleasant notions of a human lie-detector. But meanwhile I've thrown around a lot of flak so that no one will suspect what my game is and I've put in a lot of protection."

"You did it well," Watkin said. "The idea of the team alone is excellent. The right kind of camouflage. I couldn't have done better. But continue, please."

"Everyone, dancers included, is ordered to report to me if he gets approached with overtures of defection. I gently steer the approacher to Olga. After the first meeting, Anna takes her place—minus the disguise, of course. She sets a time for the run to freedom, and there you are. You have your mind-reader. Thereafter you use her as your lie-detector. All information she picks up from that, plus other sources, she relays by telepathy to her sister in Moscow. It could go on for ever."

"Why don't you use Anna as a polygraph yourself?"

"I have, and it's fine, but this idea occurred to me. It's of far greater value."

Watkin nodded deeply. "That it is. Imagine the off-duty stuff alone she could pick up. Cozily holding hands with someone and steadily reading his mind."

As Apple hadn't mentioned the touching, he realised that Angus Watkin had, after all, already figured out the secret double-act, probably from a minute analysis of everything that happened during the stage performance. Apple felt glum.

Watkin asked, "Didn't it appear to you as odd that this Porter character picked on Olga straight off?"

"I thought he was the genuine article, a star spook. But checking proved him to be a nobody. I couldn't know that he was on a Fools-rush, that he had made an emotional choice rather than a logical one." Apple smiled.

"Mmm?"

"But I'll realise, once Porter's cover slips a bit more, that he's the star I thought he was in the first place. A top man. The very one I've been looking for."

Angus Watkin lifted his cup. He sipped the tea with a light frown of disapproval. He looked like a duke in a workers' cafe. Apple relaxed and lit a cigarette.

Watkin asked over his cup, "What am I, the British, going to do with this girl Anna, knowing what she's up to?"

"You're going to fix up phony interrogations and things of that sort. You're going to feed her whatever information you want accepted as gospel in Moscow."

Watkin put down his cup. His way of letting Apple know he was still in the innings was by saying, "Have another spot of tea, Porter, while I make a telephone call or two."

"Yes, sir."

"I think things can be arranged. I'll see if Harry Wall's still available. He's our best bet."

"Is he an agent?"

"You could call him that," Watkin said. "He's working for the West Germans. They got the same idea we did—a Fools-rush. They sent in Harry Wall. I think they went too far."

Apple, smugly: "So do I."

"Kutuzov and friends saw through his cover before we did. They've been giving him every encouragement, but he's a bit dim. He may have been pulled out by now. If so, we'll use somebody else."

"What's the deal, sir?" Apple asked. He flattered by putting on the kind of expression a schoolboy unconsciously wears when looking at the captain of the first eleven.

Angus Watkin got up. "You will, if it can be arranged, be seen in dubious company by the KGB, as a starter. We have to be subtle. We can't have you strolling into the hotel arm in arm with Harry Wall."

"Of course not, sir."

"But one of the team is going out to supper with a philatelist called Household. He'll be accompanied, naturally, by the KGB."

"Will they still let him go, after everything that's happened this evening?"

"They have to. The tour's nearly over. They have to steer someone onto Olga. And they think Household is an Israeli agent. He isn't. He's a philatelist."

Apple stopped himself in time from asking, "How did you get them to think he was an agent?" He wanted to be able to flatter again by looking impressed.

He asked, "Why would they think that?"

Watkin's sleepy eyelids grew heavier. "We lost a letter in Cairo that said Household had been double checked and was definitely not allied to any Intelligence service."

"I see," Apple said. He looked impressed.

Two hours later Apple was driving a red Honda away from the Anvil. In the hotel he had made a token appearance—a wash in his room, a drink at the bar—while managing a look of despondency, although the audience, so far as he was aware, consisted solely of the reception clerk and the barman.

Before that, Apple had telephoned the located Harry Wall, mulled over details with Watkin, and rented the Honda. His call to the South African had been brief:

"This is Appleton Porter speaking."

"Hey, this is good. Great to hear from you. Are you calling from London?"

"No, here, in Edinburgh. I came up on the express this afternoon from Euston."

"I was on that train myself. Didn't see you."

"Good," Apple said. "I'm in disguise."

Slowly: "You're in disguise, Porter?"

"Right. It's for a reason I'd rather not go into over the telephone."

"Oh. I understand."

"I don't know if you do, actually. But if you'd care to meet me, I can explain. I think it's about time you and I put our cards on the table." Apple loved the dialogue.

Harry Wall said, again slowly, "Sure, sure. I can meet you right now. Just name the place."

Apple did, adding, "But not now. At ten-thirty. Now I have to see a stamp collector. Until later, then."

It was twenty past ten as Apple drove along a main street near the centre of town. There were few cars and fewer pedestrians. Apple had no trouble with directions: he had studied a map at the police station.

Ahead he saw a flashing light, yellow for caution. He slowed. Drawing closer he saw that the light topped a barrier painted in red and white stripes. It lay across half the roadway. Behind it were men with shovels and a truck whose marking showed it belonged to the Edinburgh City Council. A sign said DETOUR.

At the barrier Apple turned into a side street. He turned again at the first junction, where another detour sign pointed the way. After a hundred yards he steered into the kerb and stopped. He got out.

The street was lined with young trees. The houses stood well back from there. A good half of them were in darkness. There was no one to be seen. Apart from the yapping of a dog, it was quiet.

Apple paced, staying in the roadway. He wondered if the spot had been staked out; if he were being watched by the man he was meeting, plus others of the same team. He hoped so. He liked the idea.

Lighting a cigarette, aware of his self-conscious movements, Apple had a try at being clever. What if Harry Wall was really KGB, he thought, and being a West German Fools-rusher was only his cover—one which, as it happens, the KGB "saw" first. If so, all to the good. It would guarantee the acceptance of non-innocent Porter, whereas Watkin's plan was dangerously frail.

Apple had agreed that for himself to be seen in dubious company on a well-lit main road would be too blatant. Having the City Council oblige with a detour was smooth, and yes, the KGB would be extra alert because of

the unexpected diversion, but that didn't mean they were
absolutely certain to glimpse him in their lights as they
drove past—maybe at top speed, disliking the detour.

There was another problem, Apple mused. It would be
ten minutes minimum after the time of the rendezvous
before the Russians were due to go by. How was he to
keep Harry Wall interested for that long while saying
nothing of consequence?

Apple stopped pacing as he sensed a change in the at-
mosphere. But, he realised, it was only that the dog had
stopped yapping. Waiting was having its usual effect on
him.

He tossed his cigarette away and leaned on the Honda.
Refusing perversely to look at his watch, he guessed the
time as being close to ten-thirty.

A car came along slowly from the opposite direction.
Apple stayed in his lean. He watched the small, plain car
as it crawled into the side fifty feet back, halted, blacked
itself out.

Harry Wall emerged. His actions were so nonchalant,
he caught the pocket of his jacket on the door handle.

Apple sympathised, blushing faintly for the South African. He got a painful mind-picture of that faceless courier
stepping mysteriously out of a shadow at the midnight
cross-roads, and tripping over a rock.

After having twisted awkwardly to free himself, Harry
Wall closed the door with the gentleness of smothered
rage. He looked around. Seeing Apple, he came forward,
but stopped three yards away. He began to turn.

Apple, who had momentarily forgotten about his
changed appearance, said, "Hello, Harry. It's me."

Wall held still. "What?"

"It's me, Appleton Porter."

The South African came forward to halve the distance between them. He frowned to see better in the meagre lamplight. His body was tense.

"What's going on here?" he asked, tone hard. "What're you trying to pull?"

"I did tell you I was in disguise, old man."

He shook his head. "You're not Porter."

"Of course I am. Look at me."

"I am looking. You're nothing like him."

Apple pushed himself off from the car and held his arms out. Aware that the action had made Wall become even more tense, he said, "I tell you it's me. I'm disguised."

"That's no disguise, mister. That face is you."

So he wasn't KGB, Apple thought. He said, "I was in a fight. It was over Olga. You can see this swelling isn't natural."

"Balls. You're bigger all over than Porter is."

Apple pulled at his waist, showing the layers of sweaters. "I'm padded." He was musing that at least he wasn't having to keep the man dangling with a non-conversation.

But Apple was shocked into worry the next second, when Harry Wall, swinging around abruptly, said, "So long."

Apple went after him at a stride. This was something that no one had reckoned on, including Angus Watkin. Which, Apple knew, would give him pleasure later. But not now. That ten minutes he had to pad until the Russians passed, it had shrunk from endless to a flash.

When Apple had almost caught up, Wall whipped about and into a classic unarmed-combat crouch; his hands sliced. "Watch it," he grated. "I'm no dummy at the tough stuff."

Apple forced a puzzled smile. "Harry, what's wrong with you? Can't you see who I am?" He told about the haircut and dye job. He touched his face. Again he showed the layers of clothing, on legs as well as trunk. Harry Wall didn't move an inch out of his pose.

A car approached. Apple winced. But the occupants were two women. They stared in driving slowly past.

Harry Wall made his crouch taller and started backing away. "Keep clear of me, mister," he said. "If you know what's good for you."

"Harry, Harry. It's me. Remember that sandwich and a glass of milk you had when we were in the Oceansea coffee shop?"

"What was in the sandwich?"

"I didn't notice."

"So long," Harry Wall said. He turned and went walking quickly toward his car.

Apple ran, but on tiptoe. He wasn't quiet enough. Wall heard him, changed course like a dodging hare and left the roadway. Apple caught him up on the pavement; caught him before he had a chance to fall into his crouch.

There was an amateurish fumbling on both sides, a melee of arms and grappling hands, Apple laughing, the South African snapping, "Get the hell away from me."

Headlights came into view along the street. Where the two men were, they wouldn't be seen. There were parked cars in the way. Apple stopped laughing.

Using two hands he grabbed Wall's wrist, swung him around and got his arm up behind his back in the policeman's come-along hold.

"Bastard," Wall gasped, but he calmed to stillness to ease the pressure on his shoulder-joint.

Apple drew him toward the roadway, which was bright from the coming headlights. "Over here, Harry. I want you to take a good look at my face. Then you can stop all this nonsense."

"I don't know you."

"Yes, you do." He halted on the road. Keeping a single grip on the bent arm, he put his other hand on Wall's shoulder. He edged away to the side as far as he could, which, because of his long arms, was a reasonable distance. He hoped the positioning didn't look too awkward.

The headlights dipped, and beyond the reduced glare could be seen the silhouette of a high van. Behind that, however, were more lights—of a limousine. The van passed.

"By God," Harry Wall said. "You *are* Porter."

Apple, taking a chance, eased off his holds and set himself into a more natural stance. One eye closed against the glare of the headlights, he slapped a glance at the limousine as it went by. He glimpsed the face of one of the passengers. He was a Hammer.

Getting away from the South African was more difficult than expected. He apologised profusely, time after time, between saying, "Now we can get down to brass tacks."

Apple played it wounded. Wall had known who he was all along, he said, but had pretended otherwise because he didn't trust him. If that was so, Wall said, why had he bothered to show up here? Apple said not to confuse the issue. Where there was no trust, there was no foundation for a meaningful association. He finally agreed to think it over and call Harry Wall the next day.

Driving off, Apple told himself he had definitely been seen by the Hammer, who, hopefully, would get in touch with Kutuzov as soon as possible, and most likely already had. But delays had to be taken into account. Also, it was better to have a decent lapse of time.

So that the lapse wouldn't be empty, Apple went to the Anvil. As he turned the last corner, he saw a taxi drawing up in front of the hotel. Two Hammers got out.

Things were on the hum, Apple thought, which meant that the call must have gone through.

He made a quiet U-turn and went back. On the way to the other hotel he dawdled, drove several times around a traffic island, and stopped once to wipe the windshield.

The only people outside the Black Gordon were the police. They watched Apple park and approach. One he recognised as the motor-cyclist from earlier. The man looked at him as if he had never seen him before.

Apple went inside.

Scattered about the lobby in easy chairs were a dozen guests, among them the Sickle. Incongruously, she was knitting. Her eyes didn't leave the needles until Apple stopped beside her chair. She showed surprise.

"Yes," Apple said in Russian. "The monster's here again."

"You have a talent for disguise, Mr. Porter."

"It's from watching detective plays on television."

"If I had not been told," the woman said, "I should not have known you."

"Many thanks," Apple said. "I'd like a word with Mr. Kutuzov, if that's possible."

The Sickle pursed her manly lips. "I doubt if it is."

Nicely done, Apple thought, cheerful because now he knew for sure that the call had been made. If it hadn't, there would have been a different attitude, as well as an outright refusal. The hesitance was a balance. Another neat touch was the knitting; it gave a more homey picture.

"The thing is," Apple said, "I'd like to explain about that silliness this evening. I hope Olga didn't get into trouble."

"She is young and foolish," the Sickle said. She stuffed her knitting into a corner of the chair and got up. "I'll go and see Comrade Kutuzov. Would you wait, please?"

It wasn't a long wait. Five minutes after the woman went up in the lift, the man with the silver teeth appeared. His expression was bland. He came to Apple and asked:

"You wished to speak to me, Mr. Porter?"

"Yes. Thank you for seeing me."

"You realise, of course, that this evening's performance had to be cancelled."

Apple went into his explanation-apology. It had been a spur-of-the-moment thing, he said, him running off with Olga. He would have seen her safely back to the hotel later. It was probably the success of his disguise that had made him so headstrong. The blame was his entirely, not Olga's.

Kutuzov bowed, accepted and moved smoothly away from that by asking, "What happened after the police carried you off in their van?"

"I was soon able to prove I wasn't drunk. They let me go."

"And your swollen face?"

"A fight," Apple said. "I'd rather not go into details."

Kutuzov showed his teeth. "Meaning, perhaps, that the other man is in better condition?"

"Precisely."

"The fortunes of war, Mr. Porter."

Apple nodded. He said, "I'd like to ask a favour."

"One may ask anything."

Apple said, "If permitted, I'd like to say good-bye to Olga. I've accepted, I believe, that there are too many difficulties in the way of our friendship. But I'm very fond of Olga, and I would appreciate it if you'd allow her to come down, join me for a drink."

"That, Mr. Porter, is asking quite a lot, especially in view of your actions this evening."

Apple held up his hands. "I promise I'll be good."

Kutuzov made a doubting, "Mmmm."

"Truly. I'm tired of sneaking around. That's why I'm now approaching you direct. You can even join us for our farewell drink, if you wish." He was tempted to pretend he accepted refusal, and start to leave, just to see how quickly the other man back-pedalled.

"Well," Kutuzov said, "a handsome apology should have some reward." He smiled again. "Yes, Mr. Porter, we'll let you have a little tête-à-tête with Miss Goliski in the bar here. Without a chaperone. If, that is, she hasn't already gone to bed."

"It's not long after eleven."

"We'll see," Kutuzov said. "Excuse me." He went over to the desk, used the house telephone briefly, came back. "Miss Goliski is having a bath, but she would like to see you, and will be down in about fifteen minutes."

The bar was plain and likable. It had only two customers, older men who were helping each other tell the same dirty joke. The barmaid looked as if she had heard it nine thousand times. She yawned, then patted her closed lips.

Apple sat at a table with a sherry on the rocks. The fifteen minutes had passed, but he wasn't worried. He knew that the arrangements would take time.

Anna had to get over here from the Hotel Anvil, preferably without being seen, sneak in the back way and remove her appearance-changers, re-assemble herself and be briefed by Kutuzov. Her sister Olga, meanwhile, was no doubt unaware of what was happening, and if she had actually received a call on the house telephone from Kutuzov, it was probably one to tell her to make sure she stayed in her room.

Apple sipped his drink. He had a slight headache now that he was doubling, playing a top agent who was pretending to be an innocent. Again he was glad of his choice at university.

The girl came in. She was perfect, Olga to a physical T. She had even damped the hair around her ears to back up the bath story, and when she came closer Apple could smell the talcum.

He got up. They greeted each other with formality. When she had been put into a chair, the Sister asked for a ginger ale. Apple went to the bar.

Olga and Anna were very much alike, he thought, but it was patent that this one wasn't Olga. There were small signs which were not definable, and one of size that was. The voice.

The barmaid served him. He took the drink back to the table and sat. After taking an eager sip of the ginger ale, the girl began enthusing about all the goodies she had discovered in the British Isles.

It was an excellent performance, Apple allowed. The

serious-minded woman acted her frivolous twin in every gesture and phrase. But her voice couldn't hide the fact that it was playing a part. It had that fractional difference from the natural, the change that takes place when people use a telephone or speak into a microphone or walk onto a stage. The voice can't pretend.

"But I've had so few opportunities to make more discoveries," the Sister was saying. "We're hemmed in by rules and restrictions. We're watched constantly. It's like being a prisoner."

"Is it really as bad as all that?"

"You have no idea, Appleton. They'll let you and me sit together here, but there's a man outside the door."

"It's not as bad when you're at home, of course," Apple said, playing it soft. He brought out cigarettes. The girl asked for one, as expected. She knew every nuance of her rôle, had been practicing for this moment for a long time. And any new quirk or fad of Olga's would be passed on by Natasha, confidante and room-mate.

Apple asked, "Tell me, Olga, did you get into much trouble about this evening?"

The Sister dismissed that with a quick headshake. "Where were you going to take me, Appleton?"

"I really don't know."

"I was so excited."

Apple turned at a burst of laughter from the joke-tellers. When he looked back, the girl had leaned closer across the table. She said:

"Kutuzov told me you'd come to say good-bye."

"Well, yes."

"Does it have to be that?"

"You're leaving soon, I understand."

She sighed. "Tomorrow at noon we fly to Dublin. After

that it's back to Moscow." She pulled a face. "Just in nice time for the winter."

Apple told of how cold and damp it got in Britain. He was impressed by the way his companion hid her impatience. She let him finish before saying:

"We talked about freedom, remember?"

"Yes," Apple said, smiling indulgently as if at the antics of children. "You said you'd like to stay here and get a job in a dress shop."

Cleverly: "There are many things I would like to do."

Apple sipped his sherry and waited.

"But first, Appleton, there's the little matter of getting free." She was looking at him closely.

He returned the look, frowned, eased away and began loudly, "You mean—?"

"Sshhh."

He looked around, leaned forward and down until their heads were close. "Olga, are you saying that you'd really like to stay in this country?"

She nodded solemnly. "Yes, Appleton. That is exactly what I'm saying. I'm tired of restrictions, tired of my life at home. I don't want to spend what's left of my youth in dreary old Moscow. I want some gaiety. I want some pretty dresses. I want to be stylish. I'm sick of envying the foreign women back home. I'd like to be looked at like that. Is that so terrible?"

Brilliant, Apple thought, just the right strength of tirade, the proper blend of bitterness and poignancy. He shook his head as if in warm understanding.

The girl continued to play her theme. She listed her hates about her life in Russia, but wisely cushioned the hard sell by mentioning some of the things she would miss. Her eyes grew moist as she spoke of her friends. She sparkled while evoking a picture of a future in the West.

Apple said, "I see you've been thinking about it a lot."

"Incessantly. That's why I was in a daze this evening when you took me away from the theatre. It was my daydream coming true. It was impossible."

Apple said ponderously, "Nothing, Olga, is impossible."

They began to speak in whispers. The girl asked, "Are you prepared to help me?"

"Of course. You know that. Even if nothing comes of our relationship, we can still be friends. I'd be proud to stand by you, whatever happens."

"There might be danger."

"I'm not afraid."

"Nor I," the girl said. "It's worth the risk." She shivered convincingly.

Apple said, "We must make plans."

"Why don't we do it now? This minute? We could trick the guard on the door somehow and run away. Let's do that. Please."

Apple shook his head. "We have to keep the danger to the minimum. No more foolishness like at the theatre."

"But there's so little time, Appleton. We're leaving at noon tomorrow. It has to be done tonight."

"No, Olga. We can't rush it. We need a plan. Let me think."

"It wouldn't be any easier in Dublin."

Apple resisted snapping his fingers along with, "I have it."

"Yes?"

"A walk. Tomorrow morning. Early. It's perfect."

"Explain, please."

After glancing around, Apple whispered, "They let you people take walks, I know, so long as you're chaperoned.

Do you think you could talk them into letting you have one early in the morning? Very early? Before seven?"

The Sister frowned. "The time's no problem. We all get up at six every day. But a walk, I don't know. I think a quick escape now would be better."

Apple privately agreed, but he pointed out the risks, laying them on thick. He said, "My plan's best."

"Tell me about it, please."

He told her, describing the Musselburgh road the way it had been described to him by Angus Watkin, saying she would be sure to recognise the red car he had rented, finishing:

"But if you ask for the walk first thing, how will I know if they've agreed or not?"

The girl said, "That's easy enough. You can drive by here. If the walk's on, there'll be a red dress hanging out of my window."

"Ideal," Apple said admiringly.

The girl put a hand on his. "Go over the plan again, please, Appleton, step by step."

In his room at the Hotel Anvil, after arranging with the desk to be called in the morning at a quarter to six, Apple looked at the bed and was pleased to realise that he was exhausted. He only hoped that his mind was as ready for sleep.

Toward that end, he rolled up a towel and placed it on his pillow. Lying down fully clothed, supine, he positioned the towel at the nape of his neck. This Japanese stratagem reduced the blood-feed to the brain.

Apple was asleep in ten minutes.

The telephone rang him awake. He took the call and declined the offer of breakfast in his room. "I'll have it

later, when I come down," he said. "I have some paper-
work to do first."

He splashed water on his face and was ready. Softly he
slipped out of the room into the deserted corridor. He
wondered if Olga, who was sure to be on the fifth floor,
had slept badly through worrying over the motive for her
sudden change in accommodation.

Without trouble Apple found a rear exit to the hotel.
He got to the Honda, drove away and in five minutes was
parking some blocks from the Black Gordon.

He walked the silent dawn-grey streets. He felt mysterious. His only regret was that since last night in the
police canteen he had not been in charge of the operation. Watkin was now giving the orders. On the other
hand, that meant the Fools-rush was over. He was in the
innings as a pro.

Apple stopped walking when he had a clear view of the
hotel facade. The Sister had told him which was her window. It, like the others, was dark and unadorned. By the
entrance was parked a lone police car.

Apple waited. He smoked a cigarette and avoided
thinking of hot, steaming coffee.

At about the same time, several of the hotel windows
showed light. One was the Sister's. It was six o'clock.

Apple waited. He thought about hot, steaming coffee.

To fight that, as well as a growing edginess, he busied
himself with exchanging the laces from one sneaker to another. He pulled extra hard on one lace so that it would
break and be in need of knotting.

When the job was finished, he saw a red garment flut-
tering from the Sister's windowsill. He went back to the
car at a jog, smiling.

Soon he was in the snack bar at the bus station, gulping coffee and eating yesterday's doughnuts.

Apple didn't linger. Back in the car he headed out of town, following the Musselburgh signposts. The morning was still grey, which did nothing for the suburbs.

With the city left behind, Apple came to a stretch of second-class road that ran straight for a mile or more. On either side lay unfenced woodland. There were no people, no traffic, nothing animate.

Even the birds were still asleep, Apple mused as he stopped the car on the grass verge. He was roughly half-way along the stretch of road. So as not to disturb the silence, he got out quietly. Daylight was strengthening.

Apple strolled a dozen aimless yards, turned, and then froze. From in the trees was coming a rustling sound. As it grew, birds began to sing. They, Apple thought, could also be responsible for the rustling. But no, the source was at one point only.

Someone was walking through the undergrowth.

Like rings in water, the birdsong spread. It reached the other side of the road. From all around came a chorus of whistling and chatter and squabble.

Apple listened to it while watching the trees in the direction of the rustling, about which there was nothing furtive. He was intrigued. He hoped it wasn't a farmer.

It was a young woman. She halted after coming fully into view, level with where Apple stood. Aged between twenty and twenty-five, conventionally pretty, wearing a sweater and jeans, she was so average in overall appearance that some seconds passed before recognition came to Apple.

"You," he said. "Miss Back-up."

She smiled politely. "You remember me from the plane, of course. But not from anywhere else, I hope."

He shook his head. "You've kept neatly behind your cloak."

"It could've been awkward if you hadn't recognised me. We have no signals for this."

"Whatever this may be."

The girl half turned. "Would you come through here, please? Call me Isabel."

"Listen. I haven't got much time."

"I know. Come on, Mr. Porter."

Apple stepped onto the grass. He followed the girl into the trees, around a clump of high bushes and into a clearing. There he came to a stifflegged halt.

The two men were young and strongly built. Their faces were as ordinary as their business suits. Each held a length of white cord. They were smiling pleasantly and standing at their ease.

"Sorry about this," Isabel said. "Watkin's orders."

Apple asked, "What the hell's going on?"

The men moved toward him. One said, "If you'd care to struggle a bit, it might look better afterwards."

The other one said, "A genius for perfection." He sank to one knee by Apple's feet. "Legs together, please."

Bewildered, Apple obeyed, and again when the other man asked, "Could we have the hands behind, please?"

Isabel said, "Don't look at me like that, Mr. Porter. I'm only the hired help."

The two men got to work. Mentioning the blind ex-sailor who had taught them knotting at Damian House, they quickly tied Apple at ankle and wrist. "Gently does it," one said as they eased him down into a sit with his back to a tree. "There you are."

Apple gave him a vicious look. "Too kind."

The girl told the men, "Don't forget the keys for the Honda."

"They're in the ignition," Apple said. "There, I've given you information. Now you give me some."

After glancing at her watch, Isabel gave a nod to each man. "So long, boys."

They waved casually and strolled off through the trees as if taking a break from a picnic. The girl came and squatted beside Apple. "Would you like a cigarette?"

"Information."

"I hope you're not too uncomfortable, Mr. Porter. This shouldn't take very long."

From the road came the sound of car doors opening and closing. Apple asked, "Why the reluctance to fill me in, Isabel? Are you dreading the blow to my pride?"

She nodded on a smile. "That's it, I'm afraid."

"Tell anyway."

"Angus Watkin," Isabel said, "wanted you in the dark about this development."

"Why?"

"I suppose because he felt you might play the scenes wrong if you knew what happened at the curtain."

"So I'm still on a Fools-rush," Apple said bitterly.

"You were up till now. Your last appearance, in a few minutes, will be according to script."

"Written by Somerset Watkin."

"Right."

"I think I will have that cigarette, after all," Apple said. He was quietly angry at having been treated like an irresponsible youth.

Isabel knew in which pockets he kept cigarettes and matches. She got them and lit up, then held the cigarette for Apple to take a drag. He blew the smoke out in a long, long stream.

He asked, "And why am I all tied up at the office? I ought to be able to guess, but I can't."

"It's to protect your cover, Mr. Porter. Also to keep us in the clear on the defection."

"I'm a bit slow today."

"What I mean," Isabel said, "is we're not taking what the Russians are offering. We don't want their mind-reader."

After staring for a moment, Apple closed his eyes. He thought about it. Though sounding crazy, it fitted with Watkin's caution last night: "Don't blow your cover to Anna even though you're agreeing to help her skip, and don't do any skipping right then." This was no last-minute planning.

Tiredly he asked, "Then why are we here?"

"To make a balls-up of the job, first. And secondly, to cause a diversion."

"With Watkin," Apple said, opening his eyes, "there's always two sides to everything."

"Crafty's the word."

"So why," he asked after another draw on the cigarette, "do we not want Anna?"

Isabel said, "The risk and trouble don't equal the value, it was decided." She turned her head, stood erect. "That sounds like a car. I'll be back."

She left, circling the clump of bushes toward the road, moving gracefully. In two minutes she returned and squatted again. She said:

"Yes, it's our Russians. Anna pretending to be Olga and five or six Hammers. They've stopped a couple of furlongs down the road. Anna's strolling, three of the men are walking behind. Well behind."

Apple nodded sullenly. He had not succeeded in dispersing his anger, but was making a reasonable job of keeping it hidden, thus salvaging a measure of his pride. He felt as if he had been insulted in the worst way—by being laughed at.

He prompted, "As you were saying."

"About Anna, yes. Well, to keep her around just for the sake of feeding bum info back to Moscow would be a nuisance, in view of the fact that we'd have to continually set up phony interrogations and the like. But for that it would be fine. Anyway, we already have doublers that we're feeding."

"You mentioned risk."

"If we have Anna around the edges of the game, there's always the chance she'll mind-read something that we don't want her to, something of consequence."

"I see," Apple said. "So the innings end in a draw."

"Oh no. Far from it." She put the cigarette to his lips. "And another reason for not accepting the Soviet gift is that we, the British, can't be blamed for the defection. They'll never know where she is. Watkin did murmur that we might arrange for her to be seen in Peking. It could be done."

Apple twisted his mouth away from the cigarette. He said loudly, "What defection? What the hell're you talking about?"

"Hold on," the girl said. She slipped away but came back almost at once. "They're getting closer. I'll commentate the action for you."

"Who," Apple grated, "is defecting?"

"Why, Olga, of course."

"Olga?"

"That's what I meant by diversion. While the KGB are playing games here, weakening the detachment at the Hotel Anvil, we whip Olga from there. In fact, we must have her by now."

"But why the hell do we want her?" Apple asked, his voice still loud. "She's useless. Not worth a damn. She can't read any mind but her sister's."

"Fine. Our tame parapsychologist claims she should be able to do just that, at night, when Anna's drifting into sleep and, hopefully, mulling slowly over the main topics of her day. Which topics could be useful. She's Party and a Sickle."

"Fragile reasoning."

"That's only part of it," Isabel said. She fed him smoke. "First, the defection, any defection, is a dot in the Russian eye. Second, the ESP act will have to fold, and we can spread the word that it was a trick. Third, as I've said, the defector might be used to make friction between the Soviets and somebody else—which, coming back to the beginning, is why your cover has to stay unblown."

Apple said, "My head aches." He turned it at the sound of the Honda's motor coming to life.

Isabel got up and squashed out the cigarette. She looked around, chose a tree, went to it and began to climb. Eight or so feet from the ground she stopped, clamping there expertly with her legs. She said:

"The boys're reversing your car. One's keeping out of sight. Anna's still walking, a little faster now. The Hammers seem to have slowed a bit. Kutuzov's there, I see, leading his men. There's about a hundred and fifty yards between them and . . . here we go."

"What?" Apple said. "What?"

"The Honda's stopped. The boys are both getting out. Now they're running back toward Anna. She's also running. The Hammers are *starting* to run. Jesus. It's a reverse Olympics, or who can run the slowest—except for Anna. And she's good. Too good. The boys have to do something. There! Sid's tripped. George is falling over him. God, the acting is just awful. The other KGBs have got out of the limousine. Anna's still running. She's going to make it. *Do* something, boys. Ah!"

"What? What?"

Isabel said, "The boys are up. They're pretending to be scared of the Hammers. They've turned. They're running back to the car. Anna's chasing after them like a demon. Jesus, I think she's gaining. Come *on*, boys. Yes! They've done it. They've reached the car. They're getting in. They're driving off." She laughed softly. "It's all over."

Apple, laying his head back against the tree trunk, relaxed from his frustration. That had been the final indignity, not being allowed to watch the curtain scene.

But he was forced to admit that Watkin had made a sensible decision in respect of the twins. If Anna, in Moscow, read her sister's mind, which she was sure to do, she would get a lot of hem-lines and patterns; Olga, being no good as a lie-detector, wouldn't get anywhere near the game's fringes. Anna's own career as a human polygraph was surely damaged; there was the danger of any information thus gained being picked up from her near-sleep mind by Olga. It was neat. But Apple was still angry. And he didn't like the moral angle.

"Let me help you," Isabel said. She had come down the tree and was standing beside him.

He asked, "At the Anvil, was it a snatch or was Olga expected to come willingly?"

"I don't have that info. However, knowing Angus Watkin, would it make any difference?" Bending, she took him under the arms. "Up we go."

He got to his feet. "Now what?"

"Now you go out there and screw your cover on tight. You know what to do." Turning away from the direction of the road, she walked off with a quiet call of, "Good morning, Mr. Porter." She went from sight.

Apple, body in a crouch, made a tentative hop. He maintained his balance. Shunting around the right way, he started hopping in earnest. He got in three good bounds before he fell.

His mood in no way improved, he rolled to a tree and squirmed his shoulders on the trunk to get himself erect again. He took small hops. They carried him through the trees and as far as the grass verge, where he again pitched forward onto his face.

He flopped over onto his back, raised his head, shouted, "Hey there! Help!"

The Russians were grouped together a hundred feet away. They looked over. Anna made as if to come forward. Kutuzov put a staying hand on her arm. He and two of the Hammers started across, the latter pair hurrying.

Apple struggled. He worried his wrists against the cord to make some convincing signs of friction. When it began to hurt too much, he gave up. He thought he had taken quite enough punishment during this innings, which was no longer his in any case.

The Hammers arrived. They crouched beside him and set to work on the knots. Apple remembered that the

blind ex-sailor at Damian House had taught Eastern knotting as well as Western, Arabian, Norse and Amerindian,
and he hoped Isabel's boys had born that in mind. He was
eager to find fault.

The Hammers were well trained. They neither asked
questions nor showed interest. They might have been un-
tying a parcel for somebody else.

The man with the silver teeth was equally stone-faced.
He stopped nearby and listened placidly as Apple began
to fume and rant—thus giving freedom to his anger.

He would go to the police. This was an outrage. He
was a British subject. They couldn't get away with it.
They couldn't treat people in this country the way they
did in Russia. There were laws here to protect the indi-
vidual.

Into a gap, Kutuzov asked, "Are you under the impression, Mr. Porter, that *we* tied you up?"

"Somebody did."

"We had nothing whatever to do with it, as I'm sure
you must realise."

The cords off, Apple sat up. He rubbed his wrists and
ankles. "I'm finished with all this, with all you people. I
want nothing more to do with any of you, Olga included."

"Calm yourself, my friend."

"Calm myself?" Apple asked, glaring upward. "How
would you like to be assaulted and trussed up like a pig in
a market?"

"Who were these people?" Kutuzov said. "And what
were you doing out here on this particular road?" He
raised a squat hand. "But of course. Olga has been
naughtier than I thought."

"That's one way of putting it," Apple huffed. He looked
around. "Where's my car?"

"I have no idea, I assure you."

"I doubt that."

"My word of honour."

Apple got up. He folded his arms belligerently and stared down at the other man. "You know what I think?"

"Tell me, Mr. Porter."

"I think you're all a bunch of spies."

Kutuzov touched his wart and murmured, "Really?"

"Yes. Every one of you. I can see it all now. I've been a fool. A reporter called Jim Donald, *he's* a spy. That policeman who accused me of being drunk, *he's* a spy. A man I talked to last night, name of Harry Wall, *he's* a spy. You're all spies and I wash my hands of you completely."

"You exaggerate, my friend. You're overwrought, as well as being a victim of the Western television drug. Spies indeed."

Apple said hotly, "It's true, it's true."

"And little Olga?"

"Even she, yes. All of you."

The man with the silver teeth asked, "Whom did you say the people were who tied you up?"

"I didn't say. I don't know. I'll leave that problem to the police. It was a criminal act. I shall report it at once." He flung his arms down from their fold and moved away. "Good-bye."

Ahead, the limousine had been brought up to join the waiting group. Anna stood with her head down. Apple wondered who would get the lion's share of blame for the fiasco.

Following him, Kutuzov said, "You must allow us to give you a lift into town, Mr. Porter."

"No, thank you," Apple said stiffly. "To repeat myself, I

want nothing more to do with you people. It's possible that I'm lucky to be still alive."

Kutuzov said, "How you do exaggerate."

Apple didn't answer. He was near the others now and his breathing had gone tight.

It was possible, he thought. Kutuzov could have seen what might be planned and taken precautions. There was small risk of him losing out in the end. In case the escape came off, there would be a car waiting somewhere ahead to run interference. The plant could have been made some other time.

Apple paused near the group. He said, "Good-bye, Olga. I'm sorry about all this, but I'm through."

Keeping her gaze down, the girl said, "Good-bye, Appleton."

Apple walked on. His breathing was tighter than ever. It was with the effort of keeping from laughing.

There sounded the slamming of doors. The next moment the limousine drove slowly past.

It was the voice that proved it, Apple mused. Hers just now had been real. She wasn't acting Olga, for Olga she was. A switch had been made. Watkin had blithely snatched himself the mind-reading Anna, and didn't know it.

Like a pro, Apple didn't give in to his laughter until the limousine had gone from sight.